Carl Weber's Kingpins:

Penthouse View

Carl Weber Presents

Carl Weber's Kingpins:

Penthouse View

Carl Weber Presents

Zari

www.urbanbooks.net

Urban Books, LLC
300 Farmingdale Road, N.Y.-Route 109
Farmingdale, NY 11735

ISBN 13: 978-1-64556-439-3

First Trade Paperback Printing June 2023
Printed in the United States of America

10 9 8 7 6 5 4 3

Distributed by Kensington Publishing Corp.
Submit orders to:
Customer Service
400 Hahn Road
Westminster, MD 21157-4627
Phone: 1-800-733-3000
Fax: 1-800-659-2436

Carl Weber's Kingpins:

Penthouse View

Carl Weber Presents

Zari

Chapter 1

So let me tell you how it all began for me. I was twenty years old, and I was working at the Kickin' Chicken Shack in Dothan, Alabama. It's a city in the southeast corner of the state, about twenty miles west of Georgia and sixteen miles north of Florida. Overall, Dothan ain't a bad place to live; it has a good school system, shopping, and a lot of eating choices.

But I wanted out.

I had never been the best student while I was in high school. I don't know . . . Nothing that my teachers had to say was of any interest to me at all. My mind was on finding a way to get out of Dothan. After I graduated high school, I knew college wasn't in my future, so I figured I'd keep working at the Chicken Shack until I had saved enough money to put Dothan in my rearview. I had big plans to go to Miami or Atlanta, hell, even Tallahassee, but after two years I had barely saved enough money to buy a car to get back and forth to work. That was mostly my fault. I spent way too much of the money I was supposed to be saving on clothes and shoes. I had to do better. I needed a plan, or I could really see myself ending up like Miss Gina. She'd been working here for damn near twenty years.

"That ain't happening," I said aloud.

"What ain't happening?" Miss Gina asked.

"Nothing. Just thinking out loud," I said as a man came into the Shack. My heart stopped at the sight of tall, dark, and deep chocolate. I watched as this well-dressed man with deep-set and very intense eyes and full lips that were framed by the sexiest goatee swaggered to the counter.

"Welcome to the Shack," I announced. "What can I get for you today?"

He looked greedily at me and said, "I'm tempted to say that I'd like two large breasts and two spicy thighs, but I'll just have a two-piece meal and a Coke."

I know, it was a corny line, but it was kind of cute, and so was he, so I smiled.

"You want that for here?"

"Oh, yes, definitely for here."

"Your total is six fifty-three."

He reached into his pocket, pulled out a thick roll of bills, and handed me a twenty.

"Your order number is fifty-two." I handed him his change and a cup. "Have a seat, and I will bring your order to you."

He smiled. "You personally"—he leaned forward—"Jenise?"

"Yes, sir, I will bring your order to you personally."

"Thank you, Jenise. My name is Milton, Milton Holmes." He pointed. "And I'll be sitting over there, waiting for you."

That was how my story began. I didn't know it at the time, but that man and the next few days changed my life. Once you hear my story, I'll let you decide if I would have been better off taking my break and letting Miss Gina take Mr. Milton Holmes his two-piece dinner.

But I didn't go on break; I picked the biggest breast and wing on the rack and hurried to take him his food.

"Here's your order, sir."

"Milton."

"Two-piece dinner," I said, smiling flirtatiously but doing my best to treat him professionally, like I would any other customer. "Would you like a refill on your Coke?"

"Yes, please." I picked up his cup and turned to get his refill. "Damn," I heard him say at the sight of my ass, and I could feel his eyes on me as I walked away. "Ain't you gonna sit down and join me?"

"No, I have to work."

"Don't you get no breaks?"

"I do, and my next break is at two," I lied. I could take a break anytime I wanted.

"Then I guess I just have to come back at two if I wanna talk to you."

"I guess you do," I said and swung my hips back behind the counter.

After that, it began to get busy, but I watched Milton out of the corner of my eye while he ate and watched me. But once he had finished his food and thrown away his trash, instead of leaving, he got back in my line.

"Can I get something else for you, sir?"

"No. I just wanted to say that I'll see you at two, when you go on break," he said, and then he turned and walked out.

Of course, I didn't believe him. If I had five dollars for every man who flirted with me and threatened to come back and talk to me, I'd have more than enough money to say, "Miami, here I come." Most men talked a good game, but I could count on one hand the ones who could back it up with action. So I was shocked, you hear me, shocked, to see Milton Holmes come into the Shack later that day.

"Am I on time for your break?" he asked me when he reached the counter.

I looked at the clock, more for show than anything else. "Is it two o'clock already?" I asked, and Miss Gina shook her head and then walked away.

"Yes, it is. So, you gonna come sit and talk to me, or you got another excuse?"

"You want something to eat or drink?"

"Coke. Light ice."

"Have a seat and I'll bring it to you," I said and watched as he backed away from the counter, smiling at me.

Since I hadn't eaten anything since I got there in the morning, I got a cup of jambalaya for myself and then I got his Coke and went to sit down. While I ate, Milton told me that he was from Birmingham, but he was in Dothan on business for a couple of weeks.

"What I really wanna know is, what is your fine ass doing, slinging chicken in a place like this?"

"It's a job," I began. "You know, until I save up enough money to get outta here."

"Where was you thinking about going?"

"Miami, or maybe Atlanta. I got a cousin that lives there, but I really haven't decided yet."

"If I was you, fine as you are, I'd go to Miami."

"Really? Why is that?"

"I know for a fact, fine as you are, you would get paid in Miami, and I ain't talking about no nickel-and-dime job hustling chicken."

"I told you, this was just temporary."

"I can dig that. But in Miami, there's no telling what you can do."

"I guess you been there?"

"Miami? Yeah, plenty of times. In my business, I travel a lot, so I've been to Miami, Atlanta, New York, LA, New Orleans, Detroit, and Chicago."

"What kind of business you in that you got business in all of them places?"

He paused. "I'm in a network marketing business." He chuckled.

"You mean like Amway and Herbalife?" I asked, just to be silly, but I had a good idea what business he was in.

"Something like that. My business model depends on person-to-person sales by independent representatives to build a network of business partners to generate sales."

"Sounds like something I should get into," I said.

"Maybe you should," Milton said as I finished my jambalaya. "What time do you get off?"

I stood up. "Why you wanna know?"

"'Cause I'm diggin' you and I wanna see you again."

I poked him in the chest. "Then maybe you should say that. You know, like, 'Is it all right if I come by when you get off? 'Cause I really wanna see you again.' Try that next time," I said, and then I headed back behind the counter.

"Next time I will. Believe that," he called after me, and then he left.

The very next day he was back at the Shack, looking stylish and paid. The day before he had worn a suit and a tie; on this day he was dressed casually, but he was all iced out. I got Miss Gina to take his order, the same two-piece dinner and a Coke, and I got her to take him his food and tell him that my break was at 2:30 p.m. that day. I made sure that I found something to do in the kitchen when he was leaving. But Milton was back at 2:30 p.m., and he went to sit down at the same table. Long story short, he asked if he could pick me up after work, and I said yes.

Over the next few days, Milton treated me like a queen. He was the perfect gentleman: opening doors for me, helping me with my coat, the whole bit. He took me to all the best restaurants in the city, and we did everything that there was to do in Dothan. We'd talk, and he'd tell me about the places that he'd been, the people he knew. And he was so funny. I was so interested in everything about him, and I wanted to be a part of that world that he painted such a beautiful picture of.

I would be the first one to admit that I was naive back then, but I wasn't stupid. I knew that the life he was painting such a pretty picture of was the drug life. It was a life that I could see myself in. I saw myself as the woman on top, the one calling all the shots. And here he was, inviting me in and showing me that world.

After being with him for a couple of days, I had figured out that the drug life he was living was what had brought him to Dothan. He never stayed at the same hotel for more than one night, he never came back to the Chicken Shack, and we never went to the same place twice the entire time he was there. Somebody was after him.

"I like variety," was what Milton told me when I asked him what was up with it. I said okay and left it alone, because it didn't really matter. I was living the life that I had always dreamed of, and this was just a taste. I was totally blown away. But there was one other thing about Mr. Milton Holmes.

We had dinner one night at Fire Stone Wood Fired Grill, but instead of taking me home afterward, as he had the past few nights, Milton looked at me and said, "I would like to make love to you tonight, Jenise."

"I would like to make love to you," I said, and he leaned over and kissed me.

He drove to the TownePlace Suites, and once he had checked in, we went straight to the room, and he took me. As we stood in the middle of the room, Milton slid his tongue inside my mouth with tantalizing strokes, his hands caressed my ass, and he gently pulled me toward him. I broke our embrace, but only for a second, because Milton cupped my breasts and his tongue trailed a path across my sensitive flesh. I moved back toward the bed. He undressed me quickly.

"Lie down," he ordered.

After I climbed on the bed, I watched as he took off his pants and stroked his long thick dick. I spread my thighs; I wanted him to have me, all of me.

He got on the bed, and his hands moved up my thighs toward my wetness. He ran his thumb over the hood of my clit. I shut my eyes as my back arched when the warmth of his lips replaced his finger. I thought I was going to lose my mind, the shit was that good. The men that I'd been with had licked me only enough to get me wet before they'd slammed it in me and pounded away until they came.

But Milton had me squirming on top of the sheets, the way he licked and sucked my engorged clit, and I felt wave after wave of ecstasy, until I thought I would explode. I let go of a scream and felt my body tremble from the pleasure that he was feeding me. As I lay there, I felt the moist heat of his mouth as he licked and sucked my lips. He raised his head, and I gazed into his eyes.

"What are you doing to me?" I wanted to ask, but no words came out of my mouth.

I wanted him inside me so badly that I couldn't think straight.

He began to pump it to me slowly. I was so wet with desire that he quickly eased his thickness in and out of me, inch by delicious inch, until he was deep inside me. Milton increased his pace, giving it to me faster, and I was grinding and pushing my hips back and forth against him. I felt myself quickly building toward an orgasm. When I felt him swell inside me, my walls tightened around him, and we rushed toward completion together. We fell asleep in each other's arms, and I thought I was in love.

So, I know that I said that I was gonna tell you how it all began for me, but I had to tell you all that first, so you understand where my head was at the time. It really began the next morning, when Milton got a phone call.

Chapter 2

"What's up, Trent?" Milton asked.

I looked over at the clock. It read 7:50 a.m. I needed to get up so he could take me home, since I had to get ready for work. Milton got out of bed and walked into the living room of the suite.

I heard him say, "Tell me something positive. I'm tired of all that negative shit you be talking."

I got up and went into the bathroom to shower. I turned on the water in the shower stall, and once it reached the perfect temperature, I stepped in and let the water caress my body. As I slid the loofah over my skin, I thought about how good Milton had made me feel. I let my hand travel down to my stomach and settle between my thighs, and I pet my mound, coaxing my lips to open. I ran my finger up and down my slit, dipped a finger inside, and felt how wet I'd gotten from just the thought of it.

Suddenly, Milton rushed into the bathroom, jerked the shower curtain open, stroked his dick, and got in with me.

"Me and you are getting outta here," he announced. Then he lifted me up and penetrated me hard, and I felt my walls tighten around him. "I'm leaving, going back to Birmingham, and I want you to come with me." Milton pumped it to me harder, and I felt him swell inside me. "I need you. Will you come with me?"

"Yes. I will!" I screamed with my eyes closed. Taking deep breaths, I held on tight as my body shuddered and I came hard. You hear me? I came hard, so hard that I almost fell when Milton let me down. My legs were so weak that he had to catch me.

"Don't hurt yourself. I need you," he said, and then he helped me out of the shower.

Now, I know what I had just screamed, but now that his dick wasn't in me, I was having second thoughts. I'd be leaving everything behind, my family, my friends, my job, and now I was wondering if I was ready for that. I knew I wanted to go; I knew that I wanted to live that life he was talking about.

So what was stopping me?

Simple.

I didn't really know this man. He had shown up in my life a few days ago and had fucked me really good, and now I was ready to run off to Birmingham with him.

As soon as we stepped out of the bathroom, Milton rushed to get dressed and then began frantically tossing stuff in his bag to get out of there as soon as possible. I, on the other hand, sat on the bed, taking my time, dressing as slowly as possible.

"You ain't ready yet?" he asked me once he'd packed his bag.

"I was just—"

"What's wrong with you?" He sat down on the bed next to me. "You ain't having second thoughts now, are you?"

"No," I lied quickly.

He put his arm around me and kissed me on the cheek. "I understand. It's a big step, just up and leaving like this. I get it. And I'd understand if you changed your mind." Milton held me tighter. "But I know you wanna go. This life you're living here, it ain't for you. You know the world is out there calling you. And I need you." He let me go, and then Milton held out his hand. "Will you come with me?"

"Yes, Milton." I nodded slowly. "I'll come with you."

"Good." He stood up quickly. "Then let's go."

I quickly finished dressing and got up from the bed. "What about my clothes? Can we go fetch them?"

He picked up his bag and started for the door. "I'll buy you all new shit when we get there."

I followed him out of the room, and then we headed out to the parking lot.

"Get in the car," he all but ordered, and then he went to check us out of the room.

A few minutes later, we were on the road. After a quick stop in Eufaula, Alabama, to pick up something in a backpack, which I was told not to worry about, Milton drove north to Montgomery, Alabama, where he exchanged that backpack for another. I didn't even bother to ask this time what was in that backpack. I just assumed that one had drugs and the other had money, and I kept my mouth shut. I guessed that was the right thing to do.

"You gonna be all right in this game if you don't ask a lot of fuckin' questions," Milton told me after he got back in the car. He started the engine. "See and don't see shit. That's how you survive in this game," he said. He pulled onto the highway, and we made the ninety-minute drive to Birmingham.

As soon as we reached his badass house, Milton rushed me through the front door, then stripped me down in the living room. He picked me up and moved over to the wall. Milton rushed to pull his dick out and kissed me right as he slammed into me, making me scream out.

"Shit!"

He sucked on my neck as his thrusts became more powerful, more intense. Shaking, I came hard on him. Milton carried me upstairs and had me stretch out on the bed. He made love to me long and slow. He began by flicking my nipple with his tongue, then gently biting it, making me feel like I would explode. I love being taken from behind, so I immediately got on my knees, and Milton grabbed my hips, pushed himself deep inside me, and started giving it to me hard and fast. Our bodies melted into one another, and before long we collapsed on the bed. He had fucked me so damn good that I fell asleep in his arms.

I didn't know how long I slept, but the room was shrouded in darkness when I woke up, and I was alone in bed. I looked around the room and saw that there was a bathroom attached. Since my clothes were on the living room floor, I wrapped the sheet around me, glad that I didn't have to go out into the hallway naked just to use the bathroom. While I was in there, I decided to shower as well.

When I came out, I finished drying myself with a towel and looked around the room. It was nicely furnished: huge TV on the wall, a four-poster king-size bed, a six-drawer dresser with a mirror above it, a chest of drawers near the door, and nightstands on either side of the bed, with fancy glass lamps atop them. All the furniture was a light elm, and to me, this color seemed more appropriate for a woman than a man, and that piqued my curiosity.

I went and looked in the closet, and sure enough, there were women's clothes hanging up in there. I'd say half of what was in there still had price tags on it, and the rest looked as if it hadn't been worn. And it wasn't no off-the-rack Walmart shit, either. These were all designer clothes. I'm talking Alexander McQueen, Fendi, Christian Louboutin, Dolce & Gabbana, and Gucci type shit. There was a La Perla long-sleeved red silk wrap robe with the 560-dollar price tag still on it. I put that on, went to relax in bed, turned on the TV, and waited for Milton to come back into the room.

I had been in the bedroom for hours, binge-watching the first season of *Bridgerton*, when I realized that I hadn't had anything to eat or drink all day. Assuming that there must be something to eat in the house, I got up and left the room. As I was coming down the stairs, I heard Milton's voice and realized he was talking to another man.

"I told you that all you had to do was be patient and I would take care of everything, right?" said the man.

"One of these days I'ma start listening to you." Milton laughed. "But thank you, brother," he said, and that was when he saw me. "There she is. I thought you were gonna sleep all night."

Since all I had on was that La Perla robe, with nothing under it, I felt a little self-conscious, but I went over to him, anyway. "I've been up for a while."

"This is my brother, Trenton. Trenton, this is Jenise Phillips."

"So, this is the one you was telling me about, baby boy?"

Milton nodded. "Yeah. She's everything I said she was, right?"

"I see," Trenton said, looking at me in a way that made me feel even more uncomfortable than I already was.

Milton turned his gaze to me. "Why don't you go back upstairs and wait for me? This ain't gonna take long, and then we'll get out of here. I wanna show you off," Milton said.

"Okay. It was nice meeting you, Trenton."

"I'm sure I'll see you again soon," he said, smiling and nodding his head slowly.

So, even though I wanted something to eat and drink, and I was feeling some kind of way about the way Trenton was looking at me, I floated back upstairs to wait, because Milton's words had made me feel so special, like I was his precious jewel.

Since he had said that we were getting out of there soon so he could show me off, I went into the closet to see what I could find that would fit me. I found a black, long-sleeved Alice + Olivia minidress that I thought I'd look cute in. I was about to try it on when the bedroom door opened.

I stepped out of the closet. "Hey, Milton, what do you think about this dress on me?" I asked, holding the dress up in front of me.

"Not Milton."

"Trenton?" I gasped as he stepped out of the shadows. I pulled the sash on my robe tighter. "What are you doing in here?"

"Milton didn't tell you?" he asked as he walked toward me slowly.

"Tell me what?" I asked, backing away from him.

"That we share everything."

"What you mean, y'all share everything?" I asked, looking around the room for something to hit this nigga with.

"Milton says you got that 'drive a nigga insane' pussy. I come to see for myself," he said and began unbuttoning his shirt.

"Milton!" I shouted as loud as I could, and Trenton laughed at me.

"What you calling that nigga for? He knows I'm up here, so he ain't coming to help you." He unbuckled his pants. "Join in, maybe," he said and put his gun on the chest of drawers.

"Milton!" I shouted again as Trenton came at me quickly.

Before I could react, he slapped me in the face and pushed me onto the bed. Although I fought him with everything I had, Trenton easily overpowered me and pinned me to the mattress. He wrestled his way between my legs and pulled open my robe.

When he let go of my hand to take his dick out, I grabbed the lamp and hit him in the head with it. Trenton grabbed his face, and I put my foot on his chest and kicked him off me. I jumped out of bed and ran toward the door. Trenton ran behind me, with blood dripping from his face. I saw the gun on the chest of drawers and grabbed it.

"You gonna die for this, bitch," he shouted.

I turned and pointed the gun at him, and I pulled the trigger.

The bullet hit him in his chest.

The impact of that shot knocked me off my feet and blew him against the wall hard. With a shocked look on his face, Trenton staggered forward a couple of steps from the wall and then put his hand on his wound. I watched the life disappear from his eyes as he dropped to the floor.

I scrambled to my feet and then stood there motionless.

The gun was still in my hand when Milton burst into the bedroom.

"You didn't kill the bitch, did you?" Milton began. But then he saw that it was his brother who was lying dead on the floor. He looked at me, and I saw the fury in his eyes. "You killed my brother!" he shouted and rushed toward me.

I gripped the gun with both hands, steadied myself, and pulled the trigger again. The impact of the shot took him off his feet, and my back hit the wall hard. I slid down the wall, with the gun still in my hand, and sat there looking at the two men whom I had just killed.

That was how it all began for me.

Chapter 3

The gun was still shaking in my hand, my breaths were short and choppy, and I felt like I wanted to cry, but no tears came out. I looked at Milton and Trenton, the Holmes brothers, lying dead on the floor in front of me. I had killed them, and now I needed to get outta there, but I couldn't move.

In my mind, I was stuck in a loop: *You killed those men, and you need to go, but you killed them, and that's why you need to go, but you killed those men.* I needed to pull myself out of it, and I needed to do it quick. I reminded myself again that I had just killed two men. Somebody might have heard the shots and called the police. With the prospect of life in prison for a double homicide as a motivator, I pushed off the wall and stood up.

If somebody had called the cops, there was no telling how long I had before they got there. I had seen enough cop shows on TV to know that I needed to wipe my fingerprints off this gun and anyplace that I thought I had touched before I got outta there. I grabbed the Alice + Olivia minidress, found a pair of boots that fit me, and once I was dressed, I got started in the bedroom. Once I got finished wiping down the bedroom and the adjoining bathroom, I thought about where else I had been and what I might have touched.

Milton had stripped me down in the living room and had carried me upstairs, but I had also walked downstairs and back up to the bedroom after meeting Milton's brother. As I went down the stairs, I couldn't remember if I had touched the wall or the railing when I went down the stairs, so I wiped them both. I knew that I hadn't touched anything in the living room, as I wasn't in there long enough either time, but I wiped it all down, anyway. As I wiped, I looked around for my clothes and didn't see them anywhere. That was when I saw the backpack.

I knew that there were drugs or money in there, but I didn't know which and thought about taking it. I quickly convinced myself that this was a bad idea. The police would already be looking for me, but if I took that backpack, whoever it belonged to would be looking for me too. That was the last thing I needed, but I did need money. Knowing that I needed to go, I ran back upstairs to the bedroom in which I had killed Milton and Trenton. As quickly as I could, I took the money from their pockets and got the keys to Milton's car. There was a black Issey Miyake shoulder bag in the closet; I got it and put the money in it. After wiping down everything in the bedroom again, I picked up the shoulder bag and got out of there. As soon as I got in the car, I started it up, but I drove away from the house slowly, like I hadn't just killed two men in there.

As I drove away from the house, I thought about where I was going and briefly considered going back to Dothan. I could just show up for work in the morning and give Mr. Williams any old story and act like this had never happened. Just like I knew taking that backpack was a bad idea, I knew going back to Dothan was a bad idea too. I had just spent the past week with Milton. What if the police investigated and found out that he had just come back from Dothan? I'd be sitting there, waiting for them to show up and arrest me.

No. I was never going back to Dothan. And I had to get out of Birmingham too. Jenise Phillips needed to disappear and never be seen or heard from again. Missing and presumed dead was what Jenise Phillips needed to be. So where was I going? Birmingham wasn't far from Atlanta, so I decided that was where I was going. My cousin Connie lived in the West End with her boyfriend, Jimmy Kay. I got my phone and started to call her to tell her I was coming, but I decided that was a bad idea too.

I rolled down the window and tossed my cell phone out. Milton had called me on that phone, so I couldn't call Connie on it. That meant that I needed to stop and get a burner, and that was when I remembered that I was driving a dead man's car. The second I saw a spot, I parked the car, got out, and started walking. I had never been to Birmingham before, so I had no idea where I was, much less where I was going. So I kept walking until I found the main road, and then I followed the flow of traffic until I finally found a store. I ducked in and purchased a burner. With the burner in hand, I walked out of the store and called Connie.

"Hello."

"Hey, Connie. It's your little country cousin." It was what she used to call me when we were teenagers and I'd come to Atlanta for family reunions.

"Hey, cuz. What's up with you?"

"I'm on my way to Atlanta, and I was wondering if I could stay with you for a minute, until I get myself together?"

"Chile, please, you know you're welcome here. When are you coming? Do you need me to pick you up?"

"I don't know yet. I will call you back and let you know."

"Is this your new number?"

I paused and thought about how I should answer her. Everything was happening so fast. An hour ago, I was about to be raped by one man, and then I had to face the sudden realization that the man I had fallen for meant to kill me and had driven me to murder. I had never killed anybody before, never even had held a gun in my hand. I couldn't even remember if my eyes had been open or not when I fired those shots. I had just pulled the trigger. Now I was trying to cover my tracks.

"Yes," I said tentatively, because I had no idea what I was doing. I was making it up as I went along. "Delete that other one and save this one without a name."

"Huh?"

"Delete the old number, name, and all, and save this number without a name," I repeated confidently, like I knew what I was doing. But I didn't. I was scared. I just wasn't about to let her know it.

"Why?"

"I'll explain when I see you."

"Okay, it's saved."

"Okay, I'll call you back and let you know when I'm coming."

There was silence on the line. "You in some kind of trouble, cuz?" Connie asked, and I wasn't gonna lie to her.

"Yes, Connie, I'm in trouble. Big trouble. Is it still cool if I come there?"

"Come on, girl. I got you."

"Thank you, Connie. I'll call you back."

Now that I knew where I was going, I needed to figure out how I was going to get there. I had been in such a hurry to get out of the house that I hadn't even bothered to count the money I had taken from the Holmes brothers. I opened my shoulder bag and took a peek at the wad of bills inside it. It seemed like a lot. Since flying and renting a car were out of the question because you needed ID, I was catching the bus to Atlanta. I used my new phone to find and call a cab.

"Where to?" the driver asked me once I was seated in the back seat.

"Greyhound bus station on Morris Avenue."

There was a bus leaving Birmingham at 11:44 p.m. that would arrive in Atlanta at three in the morning, so I got a ticket and sat down to wait. Luckily, I had to wait for only an hour for the bus to begin boarding, and while I waited, I called Connie to let her know when I was coming. I told her that since it would be late when I got there, I would find a hotel and get with her in the morning.

"I'll be there." Connie laughed. "Ain't nowhere to stay near the bus station."

When they announced that the bus was boarding, I got up and got in line for the three-hour ride to Atlanta. I was tired when I settled into my seat, but every time I closed my eyes, I couldn't escape the thought that I had killed two men. I looked out the window at the darkness, but all I could see was Trenton's lustful eyes coming at me. I could see Milton's hate, and then I all but felt the gun recoil in my hands when I shot him. I didn't want to kill them. But one was going to rape me, and the other was gonna let him do it, so what choice did I have? Either way, I had killed two men, and I would have to find a way to deal with it going forward.

And that brought me to another question: what was I gonna tell Connie? That was easy. Nothing. I wasn't going to tell her, or anybody else, what had happened to Jenise Phillips. Now I was glad that Milton had insisted we leave Dothan without me packing my clothes or quitting my job first. It made it look like I was a missing person and not somebody who was stupid enough to run off to Birmingham with a man that she had met a few days ago.

"How fuckin' stupid could you be?" I mumbled aloud.

It was for the best that naive Jenise Phillips disappeared and was never seen or heard from again. The new me needed to be much smarter and much less trusting. All I had to depend on now was myself, and if I was gonna make it and become that bad bitch that Milton had kept telling me I could be, I couldn't do stupid shit.

"Trust no one," I said, nodding my head, and that allowed me to close my eyes and sleep until we got to the terminal in Atlanta.

When I got off the bus and went into the terminal, I saw Connie right away, and I waved to her.

"How you doing, Connie?" I said and hugged her. "Thanks for letting me come stay with you for a while."

"Like I said, it's no trouble at all. I'm just glad to see you." She hugged me again. "Once you get your luggage, we can go."

"I don't have any luggage," I said and saw the look on Connie's face.

"Girl, what you done got yourself into?"

"Best you don't know."

"Okay, then. Let's go. Jimmy's waiting outside," she said to me, and she started to walk away.

I grabbed her arm to stop her. "About Jimmy . . ."

"What about him?"

"What did you tell him about me?"

"Nothing. Just that my cousin from Alabama was coming to stay with us for a while, that's all. Why?"

"Did you tell him my name?"

"No."

"Good. I'm changing my name."

"What did you do?" Connie asked, and I didn't answer her. "What name you gonna go by now?"

I had given my new name some thought after deciding that naive Jenise Phillips had to disappear, never to be seen or heard from again. "My name is Tori Billups," I said aloud for the first time.

"Tori." Connie laughed a little. "That's your middle name, ain't it?"

I nodded. It was what my father used to call me before my mother ran him off and I never saw or heard from him again.

"And Billups isn't really all that far from Phillips."

"Right."

"Tori Billups it is," Connie said, and then we walked to the car, where she introduced her little country cousin to Jimmy.

He drove us to the house they rented in the West End, and my new life as Tori Billups began.

Chapter 4

Since it was damn near four in the morning, Connie showed me to the room I would be staying in, gave me something that I could sleep in, and then she went to bed. Now that I was alone and safe inside Connie's house, I had a chance to see how much money I had. I sat down on the bed and emptied out the Issey Miyake bag and counted the bills. I had 3,745 dollars. It was a lot of money, but it really wasn't, and that told me that I had to find a way to make money.

Milton had been right about me in so many ways. I really had seen slinging chicken at the Shack as temporary, because I had always thought I was made for something bigger, something better. He had been my ticket to the woman I saw myself being.

But now Milton was dead.

I had killed him, so if I were to become that woman, I would have to create her on my own.

"Afternoon," Connie said to me the following day, when I came out of the bedroom.

"What time is it, anyway?" I asked, scratching my head as I sat down at the kitchen table.

"It's going on three o'clock."

"I must have needed the rest. Thank you for letting me stay with y'all for a while. I got some money, so I can pay my way."

Connie shook her head. "You hold on to your money. I don't know what you got yourself into—"

"Best you don't know."

"And I can respect that. All I'm saying is while you're lying low or hiding out, or whatever it is you're doing, I got you covered." She chuckled. "As long as I got a roof over my head, you got one over yours."

"Thank you, Connie, and thank Jimmy for me."

"So, what are you gonna do?"

"Lay low, like you said, check things out, see what I wanna get into. But I need to go shopping. Get some new clothes."

"There's a mall not too far from here. We can walk up there." Connie looked at what I was wearing. "I don't know if I got anything that will fit you." She was at least three inches taller than I was, and Connie was a stallion.

"I'll be fine to walk up there in what I got on."

Connie nodded. "You hungry?"

"Starving. What you got?"

"I could make you a ham sandwich," Connie said, and I frowned.

It wasn't that I didn't appreciate the sandwich or the offer to make it. I hadn't eaten in two days, so the ham sammy wasn't gonna cut it. I guessed Connie saw the look on my face.

"I tell you what. Why don't you go ahead and get dressed, and we can walk up to the mall? We can eat somewhere, and then you can shop."

"That's what's up," I said and stood up to head for my room.

After a quick shower, I put my dress back on and grabbed my Issey Miyake bag, and we headed in the direction of the West End Mall. After stopping to eat curry shrimp pasta at Mangos Caribbean Restaurant, we walked the rest of the way to the mall. As we walked, Connie talked, but my mind was on the Holmes brothers and what I had done. The fact that I'd killed them weighed heavily on my mind, but what was really bugging me was how stupid and naive I had been. I mean, really, what the fuck had I been thinking? Now, looking back, I realized that taking a risk like that was the stupidest shit I could have possibly done. But now, looking back, I questioned what Milton's plan for me had been.

He was going to allow his brother to rape me, so what was this plan for greatness that he had had for me? Be a good ho and fuck who I tell you to fuck? When I imagined my future, that wasn't what I saw. If I was calling myself starting over, I had to make better choices than to pick up and jump in the car with the first muthafucka that offered me a way out. I told myself once more what I had told myself on the bus: the only person that Tori Billups could trust or depend on was Tori Billups.

As I told you before, clothes and shoes were my weakness, so I spent a chunk of that money in my shoulder bag on clothes and shoes. Somewhere in the back of my mind, I wondered if I was spending that money to rid myself of the terrible memory of what I had had to do to survive back in Birmingham. Each and everything that I did from that point forward needed to be all about me making better choices for whatever my life was going to be. I was a new person, with a new attitude; I needed a new wardrobe was the way I was looking at it. I bought so much shit that it was too much for us to carry back to the house, so we called an Uber to take us home. Once we got all my shopping bags in the car, the trunk was full and the back seat overflowed. Luckily, we didn't have far to go.

The first thing that I came to know about Jimmy was that he sold weed. While he was in the streets, Connie sold for him out of the house they stayed in. So, even though my intention was to lie low and keep a low profile, that wasn't to be. Jimmy and Connie were living that life, so while Jimmy was doing business or just making connections, I was right there with them, hanging out in the clubs every night.

At first, I tried to stay with the plan. "Y'all have a good time. I'm good right here," I'd tell them, but that didn't last. Seeing how Connie was dressed each night and listening to the tales from the club she'd tell in the morning did nothing but pull me in. After a while, I was right there with them, living the life I'd only heard about but dreamed of being a part of. So, whether I wanted her to or not, Tori Billups was getting around, making friends and connections of her own. I was a part of the world, but I needed to get in the game, because my money was starting to run low.

I had been there for a couple of weeks, checking out how they did business, when one day, while Connie was out looking for a job, somebody came to the door. I opened the door wide enough to see who it was. It was some guy I had seen here a few times.

"Jimmy here?" he asked.

"Wait here," I said before shutting the door.

Jimmy was in the back, talking to his boy Ellis. I went back there and knocked on the door.

"What's up?" Jimmy called.

I pushed the door open and stepped in. They both looked at me like I was a pork chop sandwich. "Somebody at the door for you."

"You seen them before?"

"Yeah. He's a regular."

"See what he wants," Jimmy said, and I went back to the front door.

I cracked the door open. "What you need?"

"A couple of dimes."

"Wait here," I said, then shut the door and went to let Jimmy know what he wanted.

"You know where it's at, right?"

"Yeah." I nodded.

"Go on and take care of him, then," Jimmy said and then continued his conversation with Ellis.

When Connie got home that night, she announced that she had gotten a job as a cashier at a convenience store. After that, I worked the house, selling for Jimmy, and he began teaching me the weed game. He taught me how to chop up and bag the product, then about the different types of weed and how to tell the quality by the look and smell of it. He started out paying me by the day, no matter how much I sold. I was making three times the money I had made slinging chicken, but I was moving a bunch of product for him out of that house. I needed to be the one making that money. I had my own customers, so all I was doing was expanding his business and filling his pockets, not mine. Once I had saved enough money, Jimmy reluctantly sold me my first pound.

For the next six months, I handled my own package. Although I was doing most of my business out of the house, by then, I was making enough money to buy myself a white 2005 BMW X5. I was starting to get around and was making my name known. Anytime you saw me, I was always dressed in new shit, and my hair and makeup were always done.

One night, I was at the house when I noticed that business had slowed to the point where damn near nobody was coming by. When one of my regulars did come, he had a story to tell.

"There's a guy on the corner telling people that you moved."

"No, shit. I was wondering why it was so quiet tonight."

"He tried telling me that bullshit, but I said I was here last night, and Tori didn't say nothing to me about moving."

"Thanks for letting me know," I told him. "What you need?"

"Two dimes."

I gave him three. "Good looking out."

"Thank you," he said and left.

Once he was gone, I grabbed my coat and walked up to the corner to check it out. And sure as shit, there this nigga was, standing on the corner, doing business. I don't have any problem at all with a nigga getting his hustle on and setting up shop, but why you gotta wreck my business to do yours? With my fists balled at my sides, I went back to the house, grabbed some dimes and a few dubs, and went back and set up on the opposite corner, where my customers could see me.

Once I hit the corner, it didn't take long before some of the fellas from around the way came to hang out with me and talk shit. Oh, did I forget to mention that I talk plenty of shit? Even when I was slinging chicken at the Shack, I'd be talking plenty of shit to the customers. Miss Gina used to say my shit-talking was a part of the Chicken Shack experience.

Anyway, now that I was in the street, where my regulars could see me, I did business. I was doing better out here than I would have been if I was sitting in the house. But now that I was out there, your boy across the street was looking at me crazy, because now he was not making any money.

"Ah, you!" I pointed at him. "That's what your thief ass gets for trying to steal my customers!" I shouted as loud as I could, and he came rushing across the street like he was gonna do something.

"What you say?"

I stepped to his chest and said, "You heard me. I know you were out here telling people I moved."

"I didn't do that shit. It wasn't my fault they didn't make it down there to you," he said, but that was when Jimmy rolled up in the car with Ellis. Your boy hurried up and walked his ass back across the street as Jimmy and Ellis got out of the car.

"What's up, Tori? I see you decided to hit the street for a change." It was something that he had been trying to get me to do for a while, but I had been comfortable and making money in the house, so I hadn't seen the point.

"I ain't had no choice." I pointed. "That nigga there was telling muthafuckas that I moved, so I had to come out here and take my business back."

"He did?" Ellis asked and stared across the street.

"Yeah, but it's cool. I been making more money out here."

"Just like I told you that you would," Jimmy said, but now he was looking across the street too.

"Just like you told me I would."

"You need to start listening to me when I'm trying to tell you shit. But you hard-headed like your cousin. She needs to start listening to me when I tell her that she don't need to work. I can give her anything she wants."

"She just wanna have something for herself, that's all."

"Yeah, whatever," Jimmy said, and then they got back in the car and Ellis drove off.

Apparently, he just rolled around the block, because before I knew it, they had pulled up in front of the guy. Jimmy jumped out, grabbed him, and tossed him in the back seat of the car, and Ellis drove away. I found out later that they took him to the park and shot him. After that, I began working that corner, and since he wasn't always gonna be around, Jimmy gave me a gun to protect myself.

"You ever use one of these before?" Jimmy asked as he handed me the Glock 43.

Instead of telling him that I had used one but then admitting that I did not know anything about guns—you know, the important stuff, like how to load one—I said, "I have." I put the Glock in my black Issey Miyake shoulder bag, which I still carried. It had become something of a symbol to me that I had transformed myself into something new.

Chapter 5

Now that I had come out of my comfort zone and left the house, I was definitely making more money, just like Jimmy had told me that I would. He had told me more than once that he had been selling weed for twenty years. I was barely twenty-one, and if I was gonna be serious about this business, maybe it was time that I started listening to him.

Now that I was out of the house, I was more mobile, and Jimmy began taking me around with him while he shared his knowledge of the game. When me, him, and Connie would hit the clubs, he'd leave her alone for long periods of time, while he introduced me to his people. Jimmy started turning me on to people that I could do business with, and I expanded my business. I still had my corner, but now it was only a part of what I had going.

"I see you, baby girl. You stepping up and making this money," Jimmy said to me one day.

"That's why I get up every day. To make this money," I said, with a scowl on my face, not really feeling him calling me baby girl. If it became a regular thing, I would shut it down.

"I know that's what's real." He pointed between the two of us. "I think we can do big things together. We think alike."

"If you mean that we both are about making this money, then we are exactly the same."

"Real good together," he said.

After that, I noticed that there was a slight shift in the way he treated me. Suddenly, Jimmy was always quick with the compliments. "You look nice in the outfit," he'd say. Or "Is that new? It looks nice on you, but you look good in everything you wear."

It didn't matter that Connie would sometimes be right there.

One evening we were getting ready to go out to a club, and when I emerged from my bedroom, Jimmy couldn't stop staring at me. "Damn! I know you must be driving some nigga insane," he said at the sight of me in a pair of L'Agence high-rise, coated skinny jeans and Jimmy Choo pointed-toe pumps. "I know you fuckin' me up in that shit."

I saw the hurt look on Connie's face. "That ain't for you to worry about," I said.

Seeing the crazy way Connie was looking at him, I decided I would go to the club on my own. I looked over at her and said, "I'll meet y'all at the Loft," and then I left them alone.

The argument started before I was out of the house. "That was just fuckin' disrespectful!" I heard Connie say.

I knew then it was time for me to think about moving out, because I didn't want to be the source of tension between them. I didn't go to the Loft that night. Instead, I checked into the Courtyard in Lithia Springs. When I got home the next morning, Connie and Jimmy were all lovey-dovey, acting like Jimmy crossing the line had never happened, but it did happen, and I knew that it would happen again. I was proven right the next day.

Connie had run to the store to pick up something before she and I went to a concert at Piedmont Park with some of her work friends. I had picked out a pink one-shoulder crop top and an embellished, draped mini-skirt, which I'd decided to wear with a pair of Badgley

Mischka sandals that I thought I looked cute in. I had just changed into my outfit and come out of my room when Jimmy cornered me.

"You know, me and you could be doing bigger things together," he said, with his arm on the wall, blocking my path.

"What's stopping us?"

"I mean, if we were together, just you and me," he said just as Connie came back into the house. Jimmy jumped back.

"What the fuck is going on here?" Connie asked.

"It's not what it looks like," Jimmy told her.

I shook my head. "No, Connie, it's exactly what it looks like, and you know it ain't me," I said as I moved around Jimmy.

For the second time in as many days, I left Connie alone with Jimmy. Since we were supposed to be going to a concert at Piedmont Park, I sent her a text. She replied that I should go without her and have a good time. Since I didn't feel like hanging out with her work friends, I found my own spot and settled in to enjoy the concert. After a while, some people came and set up near me. They were nice, and before the night was out, I had a new customer. When the show was over, I ended up back at the Courtyard in Lithia Springs. It was after two in the morning when my cell rang. I answered it.

"Hey, Connie."

"Where are you?"

"I'm at the Courtyard in Lithia Springs."

"I need you to come get me."

"Where are you?" I asked, dragging myself out of bed.

"I'm standing outside the Popeyes on Lee Street."

"I'm on my way."

On the way back to the Courtyard, Connie told me that she had had enough of Jimmy's shit. It was over between them, and we needed to move out. She had already talked to a friend of hers named Marcellette, who lived in Decatur, and we could stay there until we figured something out.

The following day, we were at Jimmy's house to pack up our stuff. Jimmy wasn't there when we got there, and he didn't show up while we were packing. I had hoped that he would be there, so he and I could talk. I needed to know how their breaking up was going to affect our business. I may have had no interest in sleeping with the man, but I was definitely down to make that money with him. As far as I was concerned, what was going on with them had nothing to do with business.

Once we got settled at Marcellette's, I rolled by my corner and quickly found that it was no longer my corner. I had seen them before; they were little niggas who hung around Jimmy. They were on me before I was out of the car good.

"What you doing here?" one of them barked.

"This my spot."

"It ain't yours no more. This spot belongs to Jimmy. You was just working it for him," he said, with his hand on his gun. Knowing what the smart play was, I put up my hands and got back in the car. As I drove away, I took out my phone to call Jimmy.

"What you want?" he muttered when he picked up.

"I wanna know what's up."

"What's up with what?"

"With business?"

"You and me ain't got no business," Jimmy said and ended the call.

Chapter 6

"What did he say?" Connie asked when I told her what had happened.

"He said, 'You and me ain't got no business,' and then he hung up."

"I'm sorry."

"What you got to be sorry about? You didn't do anything."

"I know. But because of me, you're out of business."

"First off, as I said, you didn't do anything. This was all on Jimmy and what he did." I shook my head. "It should be me that's apologizing to you for coming between y'all."

"Now it's me that needs to tell you that you didn't do anything." Connie chuckled. "He tried to blame it on you."

"Me?"

"He was trying to say that you were coming on to him."

"It wasn't even like that," I protested.

"I know. I saw the way he looked at you from the first time he saw you."

"I didn't even know. I thought he was cool, just trying to show me the game."

Connie shook her head. "I was just eye candy to him. But you, he saw something in you, said you was gonna make serious money in this business."

"He used to tell me the same shit, but I had a lot to learn, and that was all I thought was going on between us. I was your little country cousin, and he was showing me the game."

"He was grooming you to be his woman right in front of my face, the disrespectful bastard. I am better off without that muthafucka. But that don't change shit." Connie took a deep breath. "What you gonna do?" she asked me as Marcellette came into the living room, dressed in a red Alice + Olivia Havana sleeveless cutout minidress and Gia Borghini thigh-high wedge boots. Now I ain't into women, but Marcellette was drop-dead fuckin' gorgeous: big round ass, big full titties, beautiful long legs. She made her money dancing under the name Magnificent at a club called Passion.

"I'm gonna find somebody else to do business with," I said.

"Excuse me. I don't mean to interrupt . . ."

"You're not interrupting," Connie said. "We were just talking."

"I just wanted you to know that I put some towels in the room for you," Marcellette said.

"Thank you," both Connie and I said at the same time.

"I just wanted to say that you are welcome to stay as long as you need to. I am glad for the company." Marcellette grabbed her purse. "I gotta go to work, but you two make yourselves at home," she said and headed to the club to make her money.

For the rest of the night, I was in the street. It may not have been Connie's or anybody else's fault, but Jimmy pulling the floor out from under me was a blow. And it couldn't have happened at a worse time. I was trying to expand, so I had put some product in the street. I needed to find somebody new to do business with, so I needed to put together as much cash as I could as fast as I could.

After a long night in the street, I went back to my new home. Marcellette had said that the house belonged to her parents. They had moved to Florida and had left her the house. She'd said that she used to rent it out, but she'd got tired of having to fix the place up after every tenant moved out. The last draw was having to replace a wall after fighting tenants had made a hole in it. It was a three-bedroom ranch-style house, so both me and Connie had a room of our own.

It was early in the morning when I got there, so I came into the house quietly. Connie was asleep, and Marcellette wasn't home yet, so I went into my bedroom and closed the door. The following morning, when I came out of my room, as expected, Connie was gone. She had gotten a job as a cashier at a convenience store, and she was so reliable and hardworking that they wanted to interview her for an assistant manager position at another store.

I was hungry, and since Marcellette had said to make myself at home, I went into the kitchen to see if there was anything to eat. I looked in the refrigerator; with the exception of a couple of bottles of water and fast-food leftovers, it was empty. I closed the refrigerator and turned to see Marcellette standing there.

"Ain't no food in there," she laughed. "If you wanna eat something, we can order or go eat somewhere."

"Let's go get something to eat," I said, and we decided to go to IHOP in Lithonia.

After we both changed, we headed out. At IHOP I had the T-bone with eggs, and Marcellette got the Smokehouse Combo. Since we had met only the day before, I didn't think we'd have much to talk about, but I didn't know Marcellette. My girl could talk, and she was funny.

"Oh, yeah," she said at the end of a story about two dancers fighting over a man. Then she switched topics. "I didn't mean to be listening in on your conversation, but I heard you saying that you needed to find somebody new to do business with."

"That's right."

"I may know somebody who could put you on to some-body. If nothing else, it may turn out to be good for you. Him and his boy smoke a gang of weed."

"Get me in front of him."

"He's usually at the club every night. I will call you tonight, when he's there."

"Thank you, Marcellette," I said as our server brought our food.

It was three the next morning, and I was about to call it a night and head in when I got a text from Marcellette saying that her guy was at the club and wanted to meet me and that I should bring product. From that, I knew that one way or another, this was going to be a worth-while trip. I just didn't know how worthwhile a trip it was going to be.

When I arrived at Passion, I wandered around, looking for Marcellette. After searching for ten minutes, I ap-proached the club manager and asked him where she was. He took one look at me and offered me a job dancing. He said that none of the women he had dancing there was as fine as me. It was only after I called him on the weak line and turned him down that he took me to Marcellette.

"He's right, though," she said after I had told her about the offer. "You could make a lot of money dancing here."

"I probably could, but that ain't my hustle."

"Right, right. Well, come on. Let me take you to meet Freeman," Marcellette said, and then we made our way through the crowd to where he was sitting. He, along with his partner, Jamarco, were rip-off artists who had recently stepped up to drug dealing.

"This her?" he asked as soon as we walked up.

Marcellette nodded. "Yup. Freeman Griggs, this is my girl, Tori."

"What's up, Tori? Have a seat," Freeman said.

"Well, I'll leave y'all to y'all's business," Marcellette said and started to walk away.

"Hold up, Magnificent." Jamarco pulled a hundred-dollar bill from his shirt pocket. "Dance," he said, and Marcellette quickly stripped out of what she was wearing and shoved her tits in his face.

Freeman stared at Jamarco.

"What?" Jamarco asked as he looked at Freeman and me. "Y'all do what y'all doing."

Freeman shook his head. Then his gaze turned to me. "You gotta excuse my nigga there. So, Magnificent tells me that you working that green and you're looking for somebody new to do business with."

I shook my head as I took a seat next to him. "That's right. You know somebody?"

"I might know somebody. Leave me your number and I'll get with you in a couple of days."

"Sounds good." I wrote down my number and was about to leave.

"You in a hurry?" Freeman asked.

"Not really. What's up?"

"You got any on you?"

I leaned forward. "You looking to buy or sample?"

"Depends on what you got."

I reached into my pocket and handed Freeman a quarter ounce. He opened the bag, took out a bud, and smelled it.

"That's good. You got an ounce of that?"

"Follow me outside," I said and stood up.

"I'll be back, Jamarco," Freeman called as he stood to his feet.

"And I'll be right here," Jamarco said as Marcellette ground her hips into his lap. "Handle your business. I ain't stopping you."

Freeman and I went out to my car, and after he paid for his ounce, he rolled, and we smoked a blunt and talked about the game. After that, he went back inside the club, and I went home.

A couple of days later, Freeman called me, but it was for another ounce and not the hookup.

"Me and Thimba been missing each other, but I'm gonna get that done for you," he said when he let me in the house.

"I appreciate it," I said, instead of telling him that it was going to get hectic for me soon if I didn't find somebody.

"Give me another day."

I had been talking to people, but so far Freeman was my best bet. I had even considered swallowing my pride and begging Jimmy to do business with me one more time. I knew what he wanted—he wanted me—so I wondered how far I was willing to go to make it happen.

Not that far, I thought just as pretty woman came into the living room from the bedroom, wearing the shit out of a Coperni cutout body-con minidress.

"I want you to meet somebody, Tori. This is Jamarco's girlfriend, Kendra. She's a friend of Marcellette."

"Oh." Kendra smiled. "It's nice to meet you. Me and Marcellette used to dance together at the Fox."

"Good to meet you, Kendra," I said and made my move toward the door. I drove away from there, wondering if Kendra was Jamarco's girlfriend, what she was doing coming out of Freeman's bedroom. but I knew that it was none of my business.

Anyway, the next day Freeman called me and asked me to come by so he could take me to handle my business. When I got to his apartment, Jamarco was there, all hugged up with Kendra. There was another woman there, but nobody bothered to introduce me to her. Once he told me what I was getting and how much it was going to cost me, Freeman held out his hand.

"Give me your money and I'll go get it," he told me.

I laughed. "That shit ain't happening. I'm not about to just hand you my money. I wanna meet him."

"That ain't the way this gonna work. You give me the money and wait here until I get back. It ain't far. I won't be gone long."

"No, it's not. You're gonna be about your word and take me to meet him. I don't need you taxing me."

Freeman stood there for a second or two, looking like he was insulted that I would say that to him. "I wouldn't do you like that." He started for the door. "Come on, Tori."

"And I'm driving," I said and followed him out.

When we got there, Freeman held out his hand, and we went through the same routine.

"I'm sorry, Tori, but this is the way it gotta be. Man said he'll do business with you, but he ain't interested in meeting nobody."

I reluctantly put the money in his hand. "How I know I can trust you?"

"We're outside his crib. I'ma be right back."

"How do I know that you won't walk in that building and never come back out?"

"I guess you don't know, so you just gonna have to trust me."

"That's just it. I don't trust no man. Y'all will say and do anything to get what you want."

"True. But trust that today I'm not gonna do you like that." He paused. "Okay?"

"Okay."

"I'll be right back," Freeman said and got out of the car.

I all but held my breath and watched as Freeman walked my money into the building. When I lost sight of him was when I started watching the clock. He had been gone for just over six minutes when I heard a door slam. I looked up, expecting to see Freeman coming out of the breezeway, but instead, it was a tall, slim man with long dreads. When he walked up to the car was when I rolled down my window.

"Tori Billups?"

"Yes."

He held out his hand. "My name is Thimba. I'm the one you came to see."

"Oh, okay. It's good to meet you."

"You used to run with Jimmy Kay, right?"

"I did."

"You're his woman's cousin, right?"

"I am. I take it that Jimmy used to do business with you?"

He nodded. "That's right. Any reason you ain't doing business with Jimmy no more?"

"Personal reasons," I said, and Thimba held up his hand.

"Over your cousin."

"How do you know that?"

"Some things, you know, are just a bad idea. Him spending so much time with you and you being her cousin, it was just a matter of time."

Wondering why he knew so much about my business, I said, "You must know something I don't."

"I know Jimmy." He took a step back and reached into his pocket. "Freeman's gonna be down in a minute with what you paid for." He handed me a card. "I got a shop in the West End. Come holla at me tomorrow."

"I will," I said and watched as he walked to a car, got in, and drove off. A minute later, Freeman came out of the building and headed for the car.

"So, you trust me now?" he asked the second that he shut his door. He handed me my product, and I looked inside. I took a big bud out and smelled it.

"Not really." I started the car. "You're a man, and men can't be trusted. But we're good until you prove that I can't trust you."

"I guess that's a start," Freeman said, and we drove back to his apartment.

I came into the apartment with him and smoked a blunt, and I had drinks with him, Jamarco, Kendra, and whatever the other woman's name was, because I had yet to be introduced to her. I never saw her again, but over the next few months, me, Freeman, Jamarco, and Kendra got to be really close.

Chapter 7

The next day I was at Thimba's shop in the West End. He printed custom T-shirts and sold Greek paraphernalia. I had been by there a bunch of times and had never known what was up inside. I had even gone there with Jimmy a couple of times. Of course, Jimmy had told me it was personal and had insisted I wait in the car. And people asked me why I don't trust men. But like it or not, trust them or not, it was their game, their rules, and they paid the umpires, so I had to deal with them.

When I walked into the shop, the sounds of reggae music and the heavy scent of incense mixed with just a hint of weed filled the air.

"I'll be right out," said a voice from the back of the store. So I took the opportunity to wander around the shop. The walls were filled with Civil Rights–era posters, some of which I recognized. Some of them, I assumed, featured the founders of the Black Greek letter organizations known as the Divine Nine. I was overcome by a sense of pride and admiration for what they had accomplished as Thimba came out from the back.

"Tori! Glad you made it," he said and went behind the counter. "I have something for you."

"What's that?" I asked, and he put a box on the counter. "Open it."

I opened the box to find a multicolored THIMBA'S SHIRTS AND PARAPHERNALIA T-shirt. "Thank you," I said and was about to take the shirt out of the box.

"Lift it slowly."

It was good advice, because under the T-shirt was a bag of some of the biggest, prettiest buds that I had ever seen. They were the type of buds that Jimmy used to show me pictures of when he was calling himself teaching me the weed game. I gotta admit that I did learn a lot from him. If it wasn't for Jimmy, I wouldn't be where I was, doing what I was doing, making the money I was making. But damn, it was so fucked up that it had all been about getting in my pants.

"That's that good-good. That's a step up from what you got last night," Thimba told me. "That's a sample. You try that out, and next time you come to see me, we'll talk about it."

Thimba was right. It was a step up, so I was back a couple of days later to talk quantity and price. We made a deal on weight and price that I could work with, and as time went by, we did business without any issues. After I connected with Thimba, my life would take another turn, but for the time being, everything was cool.

During that time, everything ran smoothly. Marcellette and the other women who danced at Passion became a steady source of business. I was able to meet a lot of people in the game in those days. Some would be people I could do business with, and others would become my enemies. But back then, it was all good. When there was money to be made, Marcellette would call.

"She's here," would be all she'd say, and money would just come to me.

It had been a year since I left Alabama and Jenise Phillips behind and came to Georgia. And in that time things had gone well with me and Connie both, especially after she left Jimmy. So I was a little surprised when she said that she was thinking about moving to Old Dixie Highway in Forest Park and getting an apartment.

"Why?" I asked, because we had a sweet deal where we were.

Marcellette's house was paid off, so she had no mortgage and saw no reason to charge us rent. The only bills she had were the light bill and the cable bill. I paid for cable, and Connie paid the light bill. Sweet, right?

Connie ignored my question.

"Why could you possibly want to move?" I asked, pressing the issue.

"Because they offered me an assistant manager job at a store on Old Dixie Highway in Forest Park, and there ain't no way I'm getting there on MARTA."

"Congratulations." I bounced up and hugged her. "But that just means we need to get you a car."

Connie shook her head. "I haven't saved enough money to get the car I want yet."

"How much money you got?"

"About eighteen thousand."

I looked at her like she was crazy. "Girl, please. That sounds like a down payment on whatever kind of car you want to me."

"I know, but I don't want a car note."

"I hear you. Especially now that you want us to move somewhere and pay rent."

"Like you can't afford to move and pay some rent."

I sighed. "That is so not the point."

"So, you saying that you don't wanna move with me?"

"No, Connie, that is not what I'm saying."

"Then what *are* you saying?"

"That if you wanna move and pay some rent, I'm going to move with you."

"Thank you, Tori. I'll start looking for a place for us." Connie smiled. "Someplace nice," she promised, and even though it wasn't a part of my plan, I made the move.

Now, as I said, during that time, I had been spending a lot of time hanging out with Freeman, Jamarco, and Kendra. Now let me get something straight. Me and Freeman weren't a couple, and I wasn't trying to get with him on that level. He and Jamarco and Kendra were just cool to hang out with. And besides, Freeman had plenty of women, and I believed that he was fuckin' Kendra behind Jamarco's back. But once again, I was sure that it was none of my business.

A week after Connie and I agreed to get an apartment together, we spent a whole day looking for a place. We had just gotten back to the house when Freeman called and asked me to bring him something to smoke.

When I got there and knocked on the door, Kendra answered. "Hey, Tori. Love the look," she said, referring to the Schutz Ashlee aspen-green suede slouch boots, the high-rise, stretch, cropped straight-leg jeans, and the single-breasted blazer I wore.

"This is my money green look. You headed out?"

"Yeah, I got something going on today. But Freeman and Jamarco are in there."

"Go on and do you."

"I'll holla at you later if you're still here," Kendra said and left the apartment. Just then, a frantic Jamarco came out of the bedroom.

"Kendra, wait," he called and rushed past me.

"Where you at, Freeman?" I said in a loud voice.

"Right here," I heard him say before I saw him come into the living room. "What's up, Tori?"

"Making it green," I said and sat down to transact my business.

"You wanna drink?"

"Please."

He fixed a drink for me and one for himself, then handed mine to me. "Thanks." I took a sip. "What's up with Jamarco?" I asked as I handed him his package.

"He doesn't like that the door swings both ways." Freeman sat down and started rolling a blunt.

"What do you mean?"

"Jamarco wanna fuck every other woman he sees, but he gets mad when Kendra spreads her wings."

"Most men don't like it when their woman has another man."

"And Kendra is a predator."

"She's gonna get hers," I chuckled and took another sip.

"I can tell you this." Freeman pointed at my legs. "If you gap them thighs just a bit, Kendra would be all up in there."

That wiped the smile off my face. "She's into women too?" I asked, because I had had no clue.

Freeman nodded his head.

I shook my head. "I'm not into that."

"She knows that." Freeman sipped his drink. "But if she thought you were interested, she'd be all over you."

"And you know this for a fact, huh?"

"I do." Freeman stood up and took my glass from me. "In case you haven't noticed, you're a very pretty woman. I hear it's what got between you and Jimmy."

"What's your point?"

"Muthafuckas, men and women, want you."

"What about you? How come you have never tried me?"

"Truth?"

"Always."

"When Marcellette first walked you over to me, I was like, 'Yeah, that's some pussy I plan on getting.' But after I met you, I saw something in you that made me decide that I'd rather make money with you."

"I've heard that before. More than once." Milton had said that he could see that I was bound for bigger things than slinging chicken. Maybe he had planned on bringing it out of me after he let his brother rape me.

I heard the door slam and looked up to see that Jamarco had come back into the apartment.

"Everything all right?" Freeman asked him.

"She gonna fuck around and make a nigga do shit he'll regret!" he all but shouted.

"Only if you let her," Freeman said.

"If you want shit to change, you gotta be the change, not her," I said, and both Freeman and Jamarco looked at me like I was stupid. And I guess it was stupid of me to think men taking responsibility for changing the shit *they* had a problem with was what they wanted to hear about.

"What does that even mean?" Jamarco asked as Freeman's phone began to ring.

Freeman shook his head at me and answered the call. "Hello." There was silence while he listened to what the caller was saying. Judging from the look on his face, he didn't want to hear whatever they were saying. "Thanks for letting me know."

"What?" Jamarco asked.

"That was Shemika. Bump's in jail."

"That's fucked up," Jamarco muttered.

"She said that the cops stopped him. He had an open warrant, a gun, and a fifty of powder on him. They took him straight to jail."

""That's fucked up," Jamarco repeated.

"I know."

"What we gonna do? Kendra is on her way."

"What's going on?" I asked.

"I'm thinking," Freeman said.

"Well, think fast. Either we need to get somebody else or call it off," Jamarco replied.

"I know that!" Freeman all but shouted.

"Where we gonna find somebody last minute like this?" Jamarco asked.

Freeman pointed in his face. He was about to say something, and then he looked at me. Slowly, a smile crept across his lips, and he lowered his hand. He looked at Jamarco, and then they both looked at me.

"Tori, I need you to do something for me tonight," Freeman announced.

"What's that?"

"We just need you to drive the car," Jamarco said quickly.

"Drive the car where?" I asked.

"You know Tyson and them, right?" Freeman asked me.

"Yeah. What about him?"

"We gonna rob them, and I need you to drive."

"Slow down," I said.

"We ain't got time for this," Jamarco said and began pacing. "We need to call it off."

I looked Freeman in the eye. "Just tell me what's up."

"Short and sweet, Kendra gonna be in the house. She's gonna let us know how many people are in there, where they are, and when to make our move. We bust in, take the dope and the money. Like I said, we just need you to drive."

"Or we need to call it off before Kendra goes in the house with them," Jamarco said as he continued pacing.

"I'm in," I said, and they both breathed a sigh of relief.

"Thanks, Tori. I damn sure didn't want to call it off," Freeman said.

Jamarco ceased his pacing and sat down.

I took some time to think about what I had just committed myself to. I knew I was just going to drive, but they were going to rob some heavily armed niggas, so yeah, just driving still meant taking a huge risk. So, if I was going to take a risk like that, it would have to be for more than just money.

Now that I had agreed to drive, Freeman took his time and broke it down for me. They robbed and killed drug dealers and then sold the drugs they stole. As it turned out, my girl Marcellette put them on to their marks, and Kendra got close to them. She gathered the details on their operation, and when the time was right, Freeman and Jamarco hit them. Which, to me, explained Jamarco. I was sure that it took more than Kendra's pretty smile to get that close to a man like him.

"You ready?" Freeman asked once he had told me where we were going.

"Yeah."

And that was it for the conversation. Other than him giving me directions, neither Freeman nor Jamarco said a word until we got there.

"What now?" I asked after I had parked across the street and a few houses down.

"We wait," Jamarco said.

"For?" I asked.

"For Kendra to let us know how many niggas are in there and where the stash is," Freeman said.

"How does she do that?"

"She finds a way," Jamarco said.

"Sometimes she'll send a text. Sometimes she'll call and act like she's talking to a girlfriend." Freeman chuckled. "One time she called, left the line open, and started talking to them."

"She was like, 'Look at the two of you on the couch.' Shit like that," Jamarco said, proud of his girl.

Once we had been there for about forty minutes, Jamarco started to get antsy about why it was taking so long, then Freeman got a text.

"What's it say?" Jamarco asked.

"She said that there are four of them. Two are in the living room, one is with her, and the other is in the other bedroom with a woman. Product is in the refrigerator, and money's in the cabinets. She says to come on when we're ready." Freeman put away his phone and took out his gun.

"Let's go," Jamarco said and got out of the car. He went to the trunk and opened it.

"Keep it running and be ready to roll," Freeman instructed me before getting out.

He went to the trunk, and he and Jamarco got out semiautomatic weapons and headed for the house. I rolled slowly down the street.

I watched as they walked up to the house. Jamarco kicked in the door, and the shooting started. I could see flashes of gunfire through the windows, and then the front door burst open. Kendra came running out, carrying two bags. I reached across the front passenger seat and opened the door. She tossed the bags in the back seat and got in.

"Tori?" she said, her eyes wide, as the shooting continued inside the house.

"Hey," I said, with my eyes glued to the front door.

"Where's Bump?"

"He got popped, so here I am."

The next one through the door was Jamarco, with two bags. Freeman ran out, and then he stopped, turned, and lit up the man who had followed him out. Both men ran to the car.

Jamarco got in the back seat and kissed Kendra. "I love you."

Then Freeman got in. "Go!"

Chapter 8

Freeman counted off some bills and slid them in front of me. It was money for driving that night.

"I don't want your money," I said.

He caught my eye and placed his hand on the money. "What do you want?"

"I want in."

"In on what?"

"Everything."

Freeman sat there looking across the table at me, his hand still on the money. We stared into each other's eyes, and then slowly, he nodded his head. "Okay. Okay, yeah, that may just be the move."

He counted out some more money and placed it on the bills he'd slid across to me. Then he stood up and left the room. When he came back, he had a gym bag in hand. Freeman put the bag on the table and put two kilos in it; then he scooped up the money and put it in the bag too.

"You're in," was all he said.

Now, just like I knew nothing about the weed game when I'd started, I knew less about selling cocaine. Therefore, just as Jimmy had before him, Freeman began teaching me the cocaine game. He taught me how to chop up, cut, and bag the product. And since I was trying to enter a very competitive market and I wasn't paying for the product, I didn't go hard on the cut, so I had a superior product. Now I was punching with both hands, and my people were happy about the new product line.

To hear Thimba tell it, he had the best—not some of the best. Thimba claimed to consistently have the best weed in the city. And to be honest, I hadn't found or heard of anybody who had proven him wrong. Therefore, needless to say, my business was growing, and the money was coming in faster than I knew what to do with. So, I did what I usually did when I had money: I spent it. Me, Connie, and Marcellette went shopping at Perimeter Mall.

I had just come out of Forever 21 when I noticed a woman of color who had a kiosk across the way and was doing makeup. We were on our way to J.Jill to look for a leather skirt that Connie had seen there, so I told them to go ahead and I'd catch up with them. Once they stepped ahead of me, I made a beeline for the kiosk.

"I love your eyes," the woman said enthusiastically as I got closer to her.

"Thank you." I'd always thought that my eyes were one of my best features.

"I'd look for an attention-getting eye shadow to really bring them out," she said and handed me an eye shadow palette. "I think this would make your eyes stand out." She pointed to one of the colors, a crazy purple, on the palette. Then I noticed her eyeing the Etro multicolored jersey T-Shirt and Degrade high-waist skinny jeans that I was wearing. "You need something bold that makes a statement about you and who you are," she said

I agreed about the crazy purple shadow and told her, "Let's give it a try."

"Why don't you have a seat, and I'll show you a bunch of my products."

"Okay," I said and headed to her chair.

"My name is Blaire, Blaire Elliott."

"Tori Billups."

"Good to meet you, Tori." Once I was seated, Blaire put a disposable makeup bib on me that read FACIALS BY BLAIRE. "Now, mind if I ask you a question?"

"What's that?"

"What do you love best about your face?"

"You called it already. I've always thought that my eyes were one of my best features."

"I always say, focus on your best features and work out from there."

"After that, I'd say my lips."

"Yes. And you have a diamond-shaped face, a celestial nose to go with those bow-shaped lips, so I'd start with a good foundation." She laughed. "Of course, if your complexion is flawless, you can skip the foundation if you want to."

"How many people do you know with flawless skin?" I asked.

"None." She laughed. "For women with clear skin like yours, you could use concealer where needed and follow with a light dusting of loose powder for a natural look."

"Look fierce but not made up."

"Exactly. So, knowing your skin's undertones is important for choosing the right makeup colors for you. You don't wanna go out looking any old kind of way. So, stick with the right palette."

"All right now, I can go bold sometimes when I want to."

"And you can do that. Having a deep complexion like yours allows you to wear bold shades, which can overpower women with fair skin."

"Because I love to wear my bronze, orange, and fuchsia makeup."

"There are several cosmetics brands that cater to Black women, so you can find a range of foundation shades from light to dark."

"I've been using MAC for years."

"MAC Cosmetics is a good line and is suitable for women of color of all skin shades."

"Is that what this is?"

"No. I make everything I'm using on your face today."

"Seriously?"

"Yes. I seriously make all the products that I sell." She handed me the foundation she had just applied and then motioned toward the kiosk shelves. All the moisturizers, primers, concealers, face powders, blushes, lipsticks, balms and gloss, mascara, highlighters, eye shadows, sprays, and powders—everything was marked Blaire's Cosmetics.

"I see you, Black woman. I am always glad to see a woman doing something positive."

Unlike me. I was doing something, but it wasn't positive.

I went on. "Not waiting on the world to hand you success. You gotta be out there making it happen for yourself. And you are definitely doing it."

"Thank you." She laughed. "What I'm doing *is* definitely something. On weekdays I work as an R & D chemist at a lab that develops skin care products, I create and manufacture my products at night, and I sell them out here on the weekend." With a few careful strokes, she applied the purple eye shadow.

"How's that going so far?"

Blaire raised her right hand to testify. "Truth. It is kicking a sister's ass, but I'm hanging in there." Blaire picked up a mirror and handed it to me. "What do you think?"

"Oh, my God," I said, looking at the work that she'd just done.

"You look amazing."

"I do. And my face feels so good."

"Imagine if you had time for the full treatment."

"Do you do that here at the mall?"

"No. Either you would come to my house or I would come to yours," Blaire said, smiling, because she knew she had me hooked.

"We definitely need to set something up." I paused to think. "I need to find out what night my cousin is off, so she can get one too." I knew that once Marcellette saw me, she was gonna want this cosmetic treatment too. "I tell you what, I may have a couple of customers for you."

"That's awesome! I need all the new business I can get. That way I can buy more materials to make more products and expand my business to sell online."

"Trust me. I know exactly what you mean. When it's time to restock, you need to get your money right," I said, and Blaire looked at me. "In fact, I might be able to help you with that."

I was making more money and faster than I knew what to do with. I needed something to put my money into, an investment, and this might be it. But I would go slow with it.

"How so?"

"What are you doing tonight?" I asked, answering her question with a question.

"Nothing after I leave here. Why?"

"My friend Marcellette dances at a club. If you're not doing anything tonight, I could take you up there and have you do her makeup. I'm thinking that once the other women see your work, somebody's gonna say, 'Do me next.' Then, some, if not all of them, are gonna want you to do them too." I paused to let Blaire think about it. "What do you think? You in?"

"I'm in. The mall closes at eight."

"I'll be back to pick you up then. How much do I owe you?"

"Fifty dollars," Blaire said meekly.

I stood up from her chair and went into my Issey Miyake shoulder bag and handed her a hundred-dollar bill. "That's your tip," I said when she started to make change. "I'll see you tonight."

At 7:45 p.m. I was back at the mall to get Blaire. The way I was looking at it was that this would be a good way to market-test her products before I invested in her business, so I was just as hyped about the night on the way to Passion as she was. I was right; the second Marcellette and Connie saw Blaire's work, they wanted their faces made up too. For the next hour, until her next break, Marcellette couldn't stop talking about Blaire. When the three of us finally walked into the dressing room, Marcellette was so excited.

"There she is. There's my makeup artist," she said, and Blaire got right to work on her face.

I was right about another thing. Blaire hadn't gotten halfway done with Marcellette before another of the dancers said, "Do me next."

When we left there, Blaire walked out with 450 dollars and had made a commitment to come back again. She came back, all right. Blaire came back to the club, and over the next few weeks, she sold everything that she had, and so she had more than enough money to expand. I took her out to lunch to celebrate her reaching her goal. It was only then that I asked her if she was looking for investors.

"I am always looking for investors. I would love to give you a copy of my business plan," Blaire said and held up one finger. She reached into the rag & bone cross-body bag that she always carried and took out a professionally done presentation binder and handed it to me. "This is it. My baby. Take a look at that. Have your lawyer and your accountant look it over and let me know what you think. I would love to have you as an investor."

"How many investors do you have now?"

"One. Me."

"I'll have my lawyer and my accountant look it over," I said, as if I actually had a lawyer and an accountant. "And I'll get back to you in a couple of weeks."

"Sounds good," Blaire said, and we drank to it.

Chapter 9

So, one night, I was at the club with Blaire—she was getting paid, as usual—when Kendra walked in with Freeman and Jamarco to see Marcellette. Apparently, she had a mark that she was gonna put them onto. It had been more than a minute since I had seen Kendra, but once she saw me and Marcellette, she was on Blaire. She told her, "Do me next."

I excused myself from Blaire and went to see what was up with my people. They were sitting at a table in the back of the club, and Marcellette was with them. She had indeed picked out another mark and was telling them what they needed to know. Marcellette discreetly pointed him out.

"His name is Arthur Meyer, but he calls himself Dutch Schultz," Marcellette said, and everybody laughed.

"Why?" I asked. Dutch Schultz had been a gangster in New York in the 1920s and 1930s, and he'd made his fortune in bootlegging and the numbers racket. "Why would he call himself that?"

"I have no idea," Marcellette said and then went on to tell us everything that she knew about Kendra's new friend. "Come on. I'll walk you over there."

Kendra finished her drink, stood up, and ran her hands down her Chiara Boni strapless minidress to smooth it out. She was wearing a pair of bad-ass Christian Louboutin suede peep-toe, red-sole pumps, which made her calves pop.

"No need. I got him," she told Marcellette.

I sat down and watched Kendra sashay over there, and when she walked by the table that he was sitting at, the Dutchman, as he liked to be called, grabbed her hand, and Kendra fell in his lap, with her arms around his neck.

"Touchdown," Freeman said.

I watched Jamarco watching Kendra as she talked to our new prey for a while, and then she bounced out of his lap and started dancing. As the Dutchman pulled out his roll and began throwing money at Kendra's feet, she began taking off her clothes. I looked over at Freeman; he had a big-ass smile on his face, like he was already counting the Dutchman's money and cutting up his dope. I looked at Jamarco and could feel his rage. Suddenly he stood up and punched the table.

"Fuck this shit! I'm out," he said, then stomped over to the exit.

Freeman stood up and finished his drink. "Let me go get this nigga before he does something foolish and it ends up costing us money."

"You need me to come with you?" I didn't want to leave Blaire, but I would if I had to for business.

"No. I got him. I won't let him fuck with the Dutchman. What he needs to do is find himself two or three hoes to fuck tonight and he'll be all right."

"Two or three? Really?"

"I'll get with you tomorrow, Tori," Freeman said, and then he left Passion to catch up with Jamarco. I walked back to the dressing room, thinking about how hard that must be to watch your woman in another man's arms and to watch her get naked for him. I couldn't do it, and it made me feel sorry for Jamarco. But two or three women just to ease his pain was ridiculous to me. But then again, I was sure that however Jamarco and Kendra decided to run their relationship was absolutely none of my business. So I kept it moving and let Kendra do her thing, which she was great at, by the way.

Therefore, I was surprised when I got to Freeman's apartment the night before we were set to hit the Dutchman. Kendra told us that the mark had gotten tired of her and had unceremoniously dismissed her. Although she wouldn't tell Jamarco or Freeman, Kendra told me that the Dutchman had got mad when she wouldn't suck his dick while they were riding. He had immediately told his boy to stop the car, and he'd made Kendra get out. At the time, they'd been riding in Alpharetta, a city thirty miles north of Atlanta, so she had had to make her way back to Decatur on her own.

"It can't be done," Jamarco said. "Without Kendra on the inside, it's too risky."

"True. I just hate to pass this one up," Freeman replied.

"We don't have to call off the job," Kendra insisted. "We know where the dope and the money are."

"But what about his boys? How are we gonna know who they are and how many are in there?" Jamarco wanted to know.

Kendra said nothing.

Jamarco stared at her. "You can't tell me, can you?"

"He ain't gonna have but so many men up in there," she argued, because she hated to pass this one up too, and to be honest with you, so did I.

"No!" Jamarco shouted. "It's too risky!"

Kendra got in his face and shouted, "You're a fuckin' coward!"

Jamarco reached back and was about to slap her when Freeman grabbed his arm. "We not gonna have that, but he's right, Kendra! Without you on the inside, it ain't worth it to me to take that risk. And I dare you to call me a fuckin' coward."

"Sorry," Kendra said, and Freeman let go of Jamarco's arm.

"Some shit you just gotta let go," Freeman said and went to sit down.

"That's true," I said. "But maybe we don't have to let this one go."

Freeman glanced over at me. "What you talking about, Tori?"

"Just what I said. Maybe we don't have to let this one go." I paused and looked at them all staring at me. "I mean, we know when and where their deal is going down, right, Kendra?"

Kendra nodded vigorously. "Right."

"What do you have in mind?" Freeman asked, and I told him my plan to hit the Dutchman. "I like that." He nodded. "That could work."

"It *will* work," I replied.

The following night the four of us were back together and ready to carry out my plan, which called for two cars and a Ford F-350 truck. We had just finished going over our assignments and Kendra was getting ready to do her part when Freeman walked up to me.

"You got a gun?" he asked.

"Yeah, I got a gun," I said and proudly pulled out my Glock 43.

Freeman laughed. "You call that a gun?" He handed me a gun. It was bigger and heavier than the one I had. "That's a Glock nineteen."

"What is this I got?" I asked, getting used to the feel and the size of my new gun.

"You got a Glock forty-three."

"You gonna have to show me how to use this one."

Freeman laughed. "It's just like the other gun."

"You not hearing me. I need you to show me how to use a gun." He looked at me strangely. "I just pulled the trigger, and two niggas dropped." It was the closest I had come to a confession. "That don't mean I know how to use it."

"I got you," he said and smiled. "One day you'll tell me that story."

"No, I won't."

It wouldn't be tonight, because we had shit to do, but Freeman would eventually teach me how to clean my gun, how to load it, and how to use it in that order. But like I said, tonight we had shit to do.

"When the time comes, just do what you been doing. You still here, so it must be working out for you," he advised me.

"Y'all ready to go?" Jamarco asked.

"We're right behind you," Freeman said, and we followed him out.

So, here was how it was gonna go. Kendra had told us where and when their buy was to take place. That was where she was now. Kendra had gotten to the spot early in one of the two cars and had positioned herself where she could see everything coming and going and, most importantly, not be seen. Freeman, and Jamarco set off in the other car, I followed them in the F-350, and twenty minutes later we were parked in what we called the killing spot, about a mile from Kendra's location. I set up a conference call, so all four of us were on the line.

"We're in position, Kendra," Jamarco said.

"It's quiet here," she replied.

There was no more talking until Kendra saw a car coming. "I can't tell who it is yet." She paused. "It's the people they're doing business with. They're getting out of the car to have a look around."

"How many?" Jamarco asked.

"Does it matter?" I asked, since we weren't going anywhere near them.

"I count four," Kendra reported.

"Tori's right. Stay focused," Freeman said, and then there was more silence as we waited for our prey to arrive.

"And here comes the Dutchman," Kendra sang eight minutes later.

"Finally," Jamarco said.

"What car are they in?" Freeman asked.

"Red Jeep Cherokee."

"How many the Dutchman got with him?" I asked, because now how many there was, was important.

"Four. He's got Jerrick with him, and that looks like Ledell and Rashaan," Kendra reported. She fell quiet, and we all waited for more information. "It's going down now. Everybody is all friendly and shit, shaking hands and fist-bumping. And there goes the money."

"The Dutchman?" Freeman asked her.

"On his way to the Jeep with his dope." She paused. "They're in the car . . . and they are on their way to you."

"You ready, Tori?" Freeman asked.

"I'm ready." I pressed the ignition button. "Y'all ready?"

"Ready," Jamarco said.

"I'm ready," Freeman said. "Where are they, Kendra?"

"They're turning now."

"I see the lights," I said and took a deep breath.

As the Dutchman's Jeep Cherokee was about to drive by, I stepped on the gas and slammed the F-350 into the SUV. The force of the impact forced the Jeep to run off the street and into a telephone pole. Freeman and Jamarco got out of their car, and Jamarco shot one man. Another man got out of the Jeep and was immediately shot by Freeman, and then Freeman took the shotgun from around his neck. As Jamarco shot the last man, Freeman fired at the Jeep rear lock and blew open the trunk.

Still dazed from the collision, the Dutchman got out of the SUV. He got off a couple of shots and then tried to get away from there. I got my gun and got out of the truck. I fired a couple of shots and went after him. When the Dutchman turned to fire again, I shot first, and his body fell to the ground. I ran back to the F-350 while Jamarco and Freeman got their drugs out of the Jeep. I watched as they got back in their car and drove away before I fell in behind them.

Chapter 10

"I absolutely love what you've done with the place!" I shouted when I walked into the house we had rented in Forest Park and saw the new furniture that Connie had bought for us. It was a three-bedroom, two-bath single-family brick home with fifteen hundred square feet of living space, and it had a fireplace. I had always wanted to sit by a cozy fire and drink hot chocolate like they did in fairy tales.

We had bought beds and linens that first day, and Connie had moved right in. She'd said that she would worry about furnishing the house later. I had actually slept there that night, since then, I'd been staying at Marcellette's house. My excuse, and it was a valid one, was that my business was on that side of town, so it was more convenient to stay in Decatur.

"Maybe now you'll move your stuff in and start actually sleeping here," Connie said, because we'd had the place for two weeks already.

"I just might have to do that," I said, walking around the living room and admiring the cream-colored Sand & Stable Rosalie four-piece living room set she'd picked out.

"You really should, since you insisted on paying all the rent."

"It will give you a chance to bank some money," I said and went into the huge family room with hardwood floors, which made the Buie four-piece set she'd gotten pop.

"You mean replace the savings I spent on my car." Since bus service ain't the greatest out here, Connie had used the eighteen thousand dollars she'd saved up on a 2018 Nissan Maxima. She was thrilled that she had no car note to worry about.

Connie and I hung out at the house for the rest of the night. We went to the grocery store and filled the refrigerator, and then Connie cooked T-bone steaks and grilled salmon. We opened a couple of bottles of champagne to officially celebrate our new home. And then we spent the rest of the night talking and watching TV, the way we used to before she got a job and I got in the game. Those were good days, simpler days than these, anyway. And then something interesting happened.

When Connie's phone rang, she picked it up and looked at the display. Then she got the biggest smile on her face that I had ever seen. She put the phone down, picked up the champagne, and poured herself another drink.

"Whose call are you avoiding?"

"This guy named Andre. He used to be my manager when I first started, and then he got promoted."

I punched her in the arm. "You got a man and didn't tell me."

"He's not my man. We're just talking. I ran into him at a manager meeting at the office, and we've been out a couple of times," Connie said as her phone vibrated with a text. She read it and smiled, and then she replied. "I told him that I was hanging out with you, but he doesn't believe you actually exist. He said that you're my excuse not to do stuff." She giggled. "Which was true, because when he first started calling, that's what I was doing." Her phone vibrated again, and she read the text. "He said that if you're really real, he wants to meet you."

"Call him."

Connie's smile grew, and she happily made the call.

"Put him on speaker," I said when she tried to hand me her phone.

"Hey, Connie," he answered. "What's up?"

"Hey, Andre. You said that you wanted to meet my cousin."

"Yes, I do wanna meet her."

"You're on speaker with Tori."

"Hey, Andre. This is Tori. Connie's cousin. How are you?"

"So, you really are real," he chuckled.

"Yes, I am. I'm as real as it gets."

"I'd like to meet you."

"You just did. So now I'm going to go back to spending some time with my cousin, okay? Bye, Andre," I sang.

"Bye, Andre," Connie sang the same way and ended the call, laughing, before Andre could say anything else.

It was going on midnight when Connie said that she was going to bed and she hoped to see me in the morning. After promising that I would be there, she went into her bedroom and closed her door. Soon after I went into my room, excited about spending another night in my king-size Sleep Number bed. I was about to get undressed and get in the shower when I thought about the fact that I had nothing there. No toiletries, no clothes, nothing to sleep in. So, if I was going to keep my word and stay there tonight, I would need to ride to Marcellette's and at least get enough of my stuff to get through some days. On the way to her house, I got a call from Marcellette.

"I was just on my way to your house," I said when I answered the call.

"You wanna help me make five hundred dollars?" she asked over the music.

"Sure."

"Meet me at the club," she said and ended the call.

When I got to Passion, I looked around for Marcellette, but I didn't see her anywhere. I did see my boy Morgan Gaines and my girl Dominique. While I was hanging out in Buckhead not too long ago, I noticed them. He was the bouncer, she was a server, and they were working the club, dealing to the guests. Before I left, I talked to her for a while, and then I gave her my card and a sample of the product. The next day, Dominique called, and they began working for me. All that running around, hanging around, and hand selling that I used to do . . . They now handled that for me. Since I had decided that I needed to isolate myself, Dominique was pretty much the only person on my team that I talked to.

I approached Morgan. "You seen Magnificent?"

"She was taking some guy to the VIP last time I saw her," Morgan said.

"Thanks. You see her, tell her I'm at the bar."

I hadn't been at the bar for very long when Marcellette came and stood next to me.

"What's up, Magnificent?"

"I'm awesome, but I want you to meet somebody. Get this." She giggled. "This guy said that he would give me five hundred dollars if I introduce you to him."

"Who?" I laughed.

Marcellette looked around until she spotted him, and then she pointed him out to me.

"What's his name?" I asked.

"His name is Deebo Burton."

He wasn't a bad-looking man—actually, he was kinda fine—but I really wasn't interested in men. I mean, they served a purpose: making money. But, as you know by now, I didn't trust men. And I knew that that dick was just a weapon in their arsenal to make you weak and make you start doing stupid shit. I hadn't been with a man since Milton, and in that time, I had mastered the art of self-enjoyment. For the time being, that was all the sex that I needed or wanted.

"Okay. But you get the money before you walk him over here," I said and ordered another drink.

Once the bartender had brought my drink, I turned and watched Marcellette say a few words to Deebo, and then she pointed at me. Deebo nodded, and she held out her hand. I watched him reach into his pocket, pull out a wad of cash, count off five one-hundred-dollar bills, and hand them to Marcellette. She deposited the money in the titty bank, and then she took his hand and led him to the bar.

"Tori Billups, this is Deebo Burton," Marcellette said, and she then walked away, leaving me alone with a man that I wasn't remotely interested in.

"Tori Billups." He stepped closer to me. "I've been wanting to meet you for a long time."

"It's nice to meet you," I said politely and wondered how rude I was going to be to him. But that was when I saw Freeman come into Passion.

"Can I buy you a drink?" Deebo asked, and I held up the one I was drinking.

Freeman caught sight of me and hurried over. "Tori!" he said. "Excuse me, man, but I need to talk to her for a minute."

"Excuse me. This is business," I told Deebo.

He took a step back and put up his hands. "Do what you gotta do."

I walked away with Freeman. "What's up?"

He laughed. "Nothing. You just looked like you wanted to be rescued, that's all."

I laughed. "And you were right. His name is Deebo Burton."

"I know who he is. He's one of Ralph Chapman's main guys," Freeman said.

I'd heard of him. In addition to being a big-time promoter, Ralph Chapman controlled most of the cocaine and heroin that came into the state. If you were doing business in Atlanta, chances were that you were doing business with him. Drugs we were stealing more likely than not came through him or one of his people.

"He's somebody you might wanna get to know," Freeman added.

"Not interested."

"All right, then let's get outta here. You can ride with me. I got some money that I need to collect."

"Cool. Let me send him on his way." I chuckled. "Look impatient," I said, and then I went back over to Deebo, who was still at the bar.

"Look, I'm sorry," I told him, "but I got some business that I need to handle."

"I understand," Deebo said, and I saw that he was looking over at Freeman, who was pacing and looking at his watch.

"It was nice meeting you," I said before walking away.

"Can I get your number?" he called.

"Get it from Marcellette," I said over my shoulder and kept walking, knowing that she would never give him my number, at least not for free.

On the way to collect the money he was owed, Freeman asked me a question that changed everything between us.

"You got fifty thousand dollars?"

I was caught off guard by the question, so it took a second or two before I said, "Yeah, I do. Why?"

"Because I'm about to make a big move, and I need a partner."

"What about Jamarco?"

"Jamarco doesn't have fifty thousand dollars. All his money gets spent on fuckin' around with the hoes he fucks with or on Kendra's back."

"My girl do be raggin' her ass off."

"But that's why he ain't got fifty thousand dollars to invest."

"Of course, I wanna hear more about it, but I'm in."

"It's going to take me some time to put it together. But I needed to know that you were with me," Freeman said as we got to our destination. It was a warehouse where a guy named Byrd ran gambling.

"Does that make us partners in everything or just what you got coming up?"

"No." He put the car in park. "We're partners in everything from now on. Fifty-fifty," he said and got out of the car.

We hadn't been inside for very long when Freeman saw the guy that he was looking for and headed straight for him. He was at a table, playing poker, when Freeman walked up and stood over him.

It took a while, but he finally said something to Freeman. "You want something?"

"You see me standing here, right?"

"Yeah, nigga." He looked up at Freeman. "What you want?"

"I came for my money, but now I just want you to die," Freeman said, taking out his gun. Then he shot the man in the head.

Chapter 11

I felt bad.

As hot and heavy as I was about investing in Blaire's cosmetics company, I hadn't taken a minute to look at the business plan that she gave me weeks ago. The last time I saw her, Blaire told me that she had branched out and had a few steady customers at a couple of other clubs and she was selling her products as well. Since she was still doing makeup at Passion and a few other clubs I frequented for business, I'd seen her around a few times. Each time I'd seen her, I'd told Blaire that my lawyer hadn't gotten back to me yet, and I'd made up some excuse to get away from her.

But I still felt bad, because Blaire had invited me to go with her to an album-release party that was being held the following weekend in the Plaza Ballroom at the Atlanta Ritz-Carlton. So bad that I told her the truth.

"Truth is that I don't have a lawyer or an accountant," I confessed.

"I didn't think you did. But I kinda figured it out when you kept telling me that he was looking at my business plan." She laughed. "It's only ten pages, and most of those are graphs."

"I'm sorry I lied to you. But I seriously do want to invest," I said and thought about the fifty thousand dollars that I had given Freeman.

"I tell you what. Why don't you come to the party with me? Relax, have a good time, meet some people, and we can talk about you and investing on Monday. How does that sound?"

I nodded. "Sounds good."

"But I'll go a step better than that. Why don't me, you, Connie, and Marcellette have a spa day? I could do facials for everybody, and we can go over my plan point by point."

"That sounds good, but I'll go you one better than that. Why don't you make us an appointment at a spa, we both get the full treatment, and you can go over your plan? How does that sound?"

She smiled. "I like your plan better. I need to be pampered."

"Damn right you do. We both do. So now, tell me about this release party we're going to."

"Well, it's semiformal—"

"Semiformal?" I interrupted. "You mean fancy gowns and shit like that?"

"I do."

"You got a gown to wear?"

"I have a very nice dress that I've worn only once that I plan to wear," Blaire said.

I shook my head, because that wasn't happening. Not if I was going with her. "Oh, but no, sister girl. If we're going to do this thing, we are going to be looking like fresh new money," I told her.

So, you know what that meant, right? It meant that we went shopping for evening gowns!

The next evening, we set out in search of evening gowns. Now, since neither of us had ever had the need for an evening gown, we were both surprised at how clueless we were about where to shop for one. After trying a few places that we thought might have evening gowns and not finding anything on the rack that either of us wanted to be seen in, Blaire suggested that we do our shopping online on her couch while we ate pizza.

"We're getting our own pizzas, right?" I asked her.

"We can. Why?"

"Because you like anchovies and black olives on yours," I said, and Blaire smiled.

"I do."

"Separate pizzas."

I was on my second slice of meat lover's when Blaire followed a link to saksfifthavenue.com. It didn't take her long before she fell in love with a stunning Teri Jon gown by Rickie Freeman. The floral jacquard shirt-waist gown had a sashed self-tie waist and a sweeping ballgown skirt that was finished in satin.

"That is going to look beautiful on you, Blaire."

"I think so too." She got up and spun around. "I can see myself flowing in that gown."

"I can too," I said, glad that she had found something that she liked.

I continued my search. It took a little longer—okay, it took a lot longer—for me to settle on something I liked. It was almost eleven o'clock, half the pizzas we'd ordered were gone, and we'd emptied two bottles of wine before I said, "That's it! This is the one!"

"Finally," Blaire whispered, and then she scooted closer to me. "Let me see," she said excitedly.

I handed her the laptop. "That one," I said, pointing to a Norma Kamali floral, lace open-back gown. It was intricately crafted in black and neutral floral lace, and the turtleneck gown had long sleeves, a large back cutout, and a pleated flounce hem.

"You are going to look so hot in that," Blaire exclaimed.

"You really think so?"

"With those hips and that open back, you are going to rule, Tori," Blaire said, and then she added some Stuart Weitzman Nudistsong leather sandals to the cart. I added the Jimmy Choo Azia patent leather sandals, and we ordered dresses, shoes, and accessories that would set off our outfits for the release party.

The day before the party, I rented a limousine to take us to the Ritz-Carlton. I didn't care about the expense. Blaire and I were going in style. The driver arrived right on time the next evening and whisked us off to the hotel. We headed inside and located the ballroom, which was filled with people.

The release party was for a new artist named Anijah, who sang, rapped, and could dance her ass off, but I couldn't tell you for sure. You see, apparently, there were two release parties, the one I was at and the executive party. It was at the executive party where Anijah and all the other entertainers were, and you needed a special invite to get into that party--an invite Blaire didn't have. And as it turned out, nobody would take my money to get us in.

Despite that, the release party that we were at was pretty awesome. There was an open bar, and the buffet easily had more than one hundred items on it. The food was great, and I ate until I was full. The music was good, and there was a big screen, so we could see the entertainment. Like I said, the party was pretty awesome. But I found out something about myself that night. I sucked at making small talk with phony people.

That's right. I said it.

The people that I met there all seemed so fake and phony to me, all of them bragging about who they thought they were in the world, who they knew and where they'd been. My thought was, *If you are all that, why aren't you at the other party?* My inability to make mindless small talk eventually drove me to the bar, where I planned to close out the evening by drinking as much Stoli Elit vodka as I could.

I was on my second drink when a man came up to the bar and stood next to me. Out of the corner of my eye, I checked him out. He was the epitome of the much-talked-about tall, dark, handsome, and very sexy man. About six-three, if I had to guess. He was wearing a gray Tom Ford slim-fit checkered wool suit and wearing it well. He glanced at me and signaled for the bartender.

The bartender came over and dropped a bar napkin in front of him. "What can I get for you, sir?"

"Rum and Coke," he ordered and glanced at me. "And whatever the lady is drinking."

"Stoli Elit Sea Breeze," he said, dropping a bar napkin in front of me.

I frowned. Since drinks were free, I could get my next drink when I was ready for another. And despite the fact that he was an attractive man, I wasn't at all interested in him, and as I said, I sucked at small talk. But instead of saying, "No thank you. I can get my own drinks," I smiled politely and said, "Thank you."

He turned to me. "Are you enjoying yourself?"

"Yes," I nodded. "Pretty much."

"I sense a *but* coming."

"But . . ." I paused, and I thought, *Fuck it. Be honest with him.* "But to be honest with you, this really ain't my set," I said as the bartender returned with our drinks.

"How so?"

"Too many phony people here, and I suck at making small talk," I said.

He laughed.

"What's so funny?"

He leaned closer. "I'll let you in on a secret," he said softly.

"What's that?"

"I'm here at the bar for the same reason. Too many phony people in here for me too," he said, and we both laughed. "I just came here to get one more drink for the road, and then I'm out."

I laughed. "I would be, but I came with somebody, and she's having a good time." I held up my glass. "So I'm here."

"You're a good friend." He held up his glass, and we drank to it. "Bryant Sheppard."

"Tori Billups," I said, and we shook hands.

"Nice to meet you, Tori."

"Nice to meet you too." I took a sip of my drink, and despite the fact that I sucked at it, I tried to make small talk. "I guess you don't work for the record company?"

"No, I don't. I'm an attorney. My firm did some work for the record company, and in exchange, we were given passes to the party. When nobody wanted to go . . ." He paused. "A little too Black an event for most of the partners. So I claimed the passes, and here I am."

I laughed. "And now you can't wait to get out of here."

"As soon as I finish this." He held up his drink. "What about you, Tori? I assume that you don't work for the record company, either. Not phony enough." He laughed. "What do you do?"

"I'm in sales."

"Oh, really? What type?"

"Pharmaceuticals," I said, and he raised an eyebrow. "I'm a pharmaceutical sales rep," I said to try to clean it up.

He gave me a look that said, "Oh, you're a drug dealer," and I quickly turned the conversation back to him.

"You're a lawyer, though, huh?"

"I am."

"Do you have a card? I may need to hire you."

He handed me his card.

I went on. "A friend of mine, the woman I came here with, has a cosmetics business, and she gave me her business plan to look over weeks ago and . . ."

"And you need a lawyer to look it over for you."

"Yes. Could you do that for me?"

"I would be happy to. In fact, I have access to resources at the firm I work for. I can put her plan before our evaluation committee." He chuckled. "They owe me a favor. They will look at her proposal, check the numbers, and do a complete feasibility study." He shrugged his shoulders. "Whatever that entails. But at the end of the process, they'll make a report with their recommendations."

"If you could do all that, it would be great."

"Anytime you're ready, just give me a call and we'll set something up."

"Sounds good," I said, and we shook hands on it.

"Hey, Tori," Blaire said as she walked up to us at the bar.

"Hey, Blaire. This is Bryant Sheppard. He's a lawyer."

"Nice to meet you, Bryant."

"Please, call me Shep."

"Shep it is," Blaire said, and they shook hands.

"He's gonna go over your business plan for me."

"That's good. I would love to get another set of eyes on it."

"No problem. I would be honored to review your plan, Blaire," Shep said and then finished his drink. "Ladies, it was a pleasure meeting you." He turned to me and smiled. "Tori." He took my hand to his lips and kissed it. "I'll look forward to hearing from you soon."

"I will call you this week," I told him.

"We'll get together then," Shep said, and then he was gone.

Blaire and I watched him as he walked away. "Girl, I'm jealous. I wanna get me one just like that," she said, swooning.

I watched as he reached the elevator. Before he got on, he turned and waved to me. I waved back as the doors closed, and I thought, *Maybe.*

Chapter 12

The people at the bar hit the floor, while others took cover under the tables, when two men rose from behind the bar and took aim at us. Jamarco raised his weapon and shot one of the men in the head. Freeman took out the other. Two more men on each side of the bar opened fire at us, and I dove to the floor. Freeman returned fire on them as Kendra dove down next to me. Once she and I found cover behind a table, I fired a few shots at the men so Freeman and Jamarco could find cover.

This had all started when we were riding and getting fucked up on liquor and weed. We passed a bar called Lorenzo's, and Jamarco said that there was a guy they called New York who hung out there, and he owed Jamarco a lot of money. Well, that was all me and Freeman needed to hear.

"Oh no, he don't," my drunk ass said.

"Let's go get this nigga," Freeman said, and we parked the car and went inside to get that money.

Needless to say, it didn't go well for us.

The shooting sobered my ass up quick.

Four men stood in the open and sprayed the bar with bullets as Freeman and Jamarco found cover. I crawled along the floor, trying to make it to a spot where I could get a clear shot at the shooters. When one stopped to reload a fresh clip, I stood up and hit him with two shots to the chest. The man went down, and I took cover as his partner began firing at me. With his attention diverted, Freeman shot him in the back.

"We gotta get outta here!" Jamarco yelled, then stood up and began firing wildly.

Kendra got up from the floor and ran for the door. I came out from behind the table, fired off a couple of shots, and followed Kendra out of there. We ran to the car, and when we reached it, Kendra got behind the wheel, started up the engine, and got her gun as I dove in the back seat. The door burst open, and out ran Freeman and Jamarco. Once they got in, Kendra drove us away from there.

"Everybody all right?" Kendra asked as she sped away.

"I'm okay," I said.

"I'm all right," Jamarco said.

"Well, I'm not! I'm gonna kill that muthafucka!" Freeman shouted. He talked some shit about going back there to kill New York, but Kendra kept driving us away from there. We would get our chance to kill him ten days later.

We had been invited to a pool party at Ralph Chapman's house. Jamarco and Kendra had gone to Miami for the weekend, so it was just me and Freeman. Now, it may not have been an album-release party, and the house wasn't the Ritz-Carlton, and the buffet didn't have as many items, but there was plenty of food, free beer, wine, and liquor, and there were enough drugs to get the whole city of East Point high.

The pool and the area that surrounded it were filled with people, mostly women walking around with their fake titties out. Some of them I knew from the clubs, and some were engaged in various sex acts. The shit was crazy, and I could only imagine what was going on inside the house. Freeman and I spent the afternoon sitting by the pool, drinking Ralph's liquor, eating his food, and smoking his weed.

"Ain't you gonna get in the water?" Freeman asked after we'd eaten our fill.

"Nope. I don't have a swimsuit."

"That's not stopping any of them."

"Do *I* look like any of them?"

"Nope."

"I didn't think so. I'm a businesswoman. They're the entertainment."

"True that."

"Oh shit," I said and looked in the other direction.

"What?"

"Deebo Burton is here," I said, keeping my voice low.

"Of course he is. I told you, he's one of Ralph Chapman's main guys."

"Well, I've been avoiding him, and he's been bugging Marcellette about getting my number."

"Of course he has." Freeman laughed. "That is what you told him to do."

"That is so not the point." I sat up in the lounge chair I occupied and turned toward Freeman as Deebo walked by. He was staggering drunk and damn near fell in the pool, so I wasn't surprised that he didn't see me, but I sure was glad.

"You see that guy he's talking to?" Freeman said once Deebo was at least twenty-five feet away.

"Yeah. Who is he?"

"That's Bowie Calbert."

"That another one of Ralph's guys?"

"Yup. Ralph got the Metro area sliced up like a pie, so Bowie controls the northeast side."

"What's he about?"

"He sees himself as the heir apparent to Ralph, and he pretty much is his right hand. But let me get something straight. Ralph runs shit, and he runs shit with an iron fist. Bowie and DeAngelo Robinson are Ralph's executioners."

"DeAngelo Robinson? Who's he?"

Freeman looked around. "I don't see him, but he's another of Ralph Chapman's main guys. They call him the Gigolo. He runs the west side." Freeman shook his head. "That is one crazy muthafucka. Steer clear of him if you can."

"Good advice."

"Trust me, you don't know how good it is, and you don't wanna find out."

"Understood."

"You see the guy coming out of the house with the two women? That's Cash Money Carter. Southside belongs to him, and that nigga there is Zaquan Butler."

"Him I know." I saw him at the club all the time. He and I had what I guessed was a mutual respect thing going. Neither of us had spoken a word to the other, but we nodded respectfully when we saw each other.

Freeman leaned closer. "Some of the niggas we been robbin' work for him."

"I get it," I said just as Freeman's phone rang.

He answered. "What's up?" As Freeman talked, I kept my eyes on Zaquan Butler. "Stay on him and call me if he moves. I'll take care of you when I see you." Freeman ended the call and stood up. So I stood up, too, as Zaquan seemed to be coming our way.

I looked over at Freeman. "What's up?"

"That was Jackie. She said that nigga New York is at the Holiday Inn out on Camp Creek."

"Let's go get this muthafucka," I said as Zaquan walked up to us.

"What's up, Freeman?" He turned to me. "You're Tori, right?"

"That's right."

"I'm Zaquan. I've seen you around. Good to actually meet you."

"Same here."

"You busy right now?" Zaquan asked.

"We were about to go take care of a problem we've been having," I informed him.

"Ralph wants to talk to you," Zaquan said, like none of that shit I was talking about mattered.

I looked at Freeman and then back at Zaquan. "Please apologize to Mr. Chapman, but we have to leave to take care of some business. I'm sure Mr. Chapman will understand. It's not gonna take long, so I will be back, and I would be honored to meet him then." I turned to Freeman. "Let's go," I said, and we left Zaquan standing there, as if his invitation to meet Ralph Chapman didn't matter. Because at the time, it didn't. We needed to catch New York before he came out of that room.

When we got to the Holiday Inn, Jackie, who turned out to be a crackhead, told us that New York was still in the room. Freeman gave her a big rock, she disappeared, and we waited. It was an hour later when I got tired of sitting in the car and got out to stretch my legs.

That was when I saw him coming out of the room. "There he is!" I shouted, reaching for my weapon.

"Fuck!" I heard him say when our eyes locked.

New York took off running. Freeman jumped out of the car, and we ran after him. He stopped, turned, fired, and then he took cover behind a car in the parking lot. It forced us to take cover behind a car.

"Cover me!" Freeman shouted, and I came up firing on New York.

He ran and then ducked for cover as Freeman got to the other side of him. New York rose up and fired a few shots at Freeman, then reached for cover behind a car. So now we had him in a cross fire. We raised our weapons and fired at New York until our guns were empty. New York ejected the clip and slammed in another. He began firing wildly in both directions; then he came out from cover and tried to run. I began firing at him as he ran. Freeman set himself, took aim, and fired. His shot hit New York in the back of the head. We rushed back to our car and drove away from the hotel and headed back to Ralph Chapman's house.

When we got back to Ralph's house, it was starting to get dark, but the party was still going on. Once we got drinks, I started to look for Zaquan Butler to tell him that we were back, but Freeman thought otherwise.

"If they want you, make them come to you. You said you'd be back. Well, you're back." We found a spot by the pool and sat down. "It's on them now."

We had been hanging out there for about an hour when I saw Deebo Burton come out of the house and look around. Then he talked to somebody, and they pointed us out.

"Here comes Deebo," I announced.

Freeman sat up in the lounge chair. "I see him."

"What you think Ralph wants with me?"

"I don't know. Maybe he just wants to fuck you."

"That ain't happening," I said, and suddenly, for reasons I could not explain, Shep crossed my mind.

"You don't think they know?"

I shook my head. "I don't think so. If that were the case, why would they just wanna meet me?"

"Guess we'll find out soon enough."

"Guess so," I said. The closer Deebo got to us, the bigger his smile got. He showed me all his teeth when our eyes connected. I could tell that he wanted to get with me badly.

"What's up, Tori?" He nodded toward Freeman. "'Sup?"

"What's up, Deebo?" Freeman said, then stood up and shook his hand.

Deebo gazed at me. "Ralph wants to see you."

I stood up.

"You too, Freeman," he said, and I didn't know if that was good for us or bad for us.

Freeman smiled and politely extended his hand toward the house. "Lead the way."

Me and Freeman walked behind Deebo toward the house, but it wasn't long before Deebo was walking alongside me. "You know, Marcellette never did give me your number," he said.

"I'm sorry about that. I haven't seen Marcellette to tell her it was cool," I lied, since I saw her damn near every day.

"That's what she said," Deebo said and opened a sliding door.

When I stepped inside the house, there he was, big Ralph Chapman, all six feet, five inches and 275 pounds of him. He was standing behind his desk, talking to someone on the phone. He waved us in when he looked up and saw us and kept talking. Shawn Michaels was in the office too. He hung out at a club called Diamonds and had tried to holla at me a couple of times. I didn't know that he was down with Ralph. Not that I would have treated him any differently. It just would have been good to know.

"Have a seat. Ralph will be with you in a minute," Shawn said.

"Thanks," Freeman said, and we sat down.

Deebo leaned in. "So, you think I could get that number now?" he asked, and I acted like I didn't hear him. He left the room quickly when Ralph hung up the phone.

"Sorry to keep you waiting," he said in a booming voice. He came around the desk, and we stood up. "Some people don't understand that no means no and need to be shown." While we stood there, Ralph went to the bar, picked up a bottle of Rémy VSOP, and poured a shot. "Tori Billups. Did you take care of your business?"

"Yes, yes, we did. Thank you for understanding."

"I didn't understand that shit at all. I just had to accept it." He walked over and stood in front of me with his hand out. "Tori Billups." I shook his hand. "I've been hearing a lot of good things about you." He looked at Freeman. "You too, Freeman. You been puttin' in good work for years."

Freeman chuckled nervously. "I was about to say . . ."

"But you, Tori Billups," Ralph said and finally let go of my hand, "I been hearing a lot about you."

"It's an honor to meet you, Mr. Chapman."

"Ralph. Please call me Ralph."

"Okay, I'll call you Ralph."

"I just wanted to put a face with a name." Ralph looked at Shawn. "Like I said, I've been hearing a lot about you lately." He stood there looking me in my eyes for longer than I was comfortable with, and then he said, "That's all I wanted." He abruptly walked away. "So if you'll excuse me, I have other shit I need to handle," he said and went back to his desk.

"Y'all can go," Shawn said, and we left the way we had come in—through the glass door.

"We out," Freeman said the second we were outside.

"Right," I said and started behind Freeman, but Deebo was there waiting for me.

"What about them digits?" he asked, and I reluctantly gave him my number.

Good luck getting me to answer, I thought.

Chapter 13

After we left Ralph Chapman's pool party, Freeman took me home to Forest Park and said that he would get with me the following day. I had an eight o'clock appointment for a mani-pedi at Gorgeous Nails on Forest Parkway, so I would get with him after that. However, in the morning, right before I was getting ready to leave, Freeman called. I told him where I was going, and he said that he would meet me there. I saw his car parked in front of the salon when I got there. When I went inside, Freeman was just putting his feet in the basin of water at his chair. I waved when he saw me.

"Tori Billups. I have an eight o'clock appointment," I told the woman at the front desk.

"You sign and pick polish," she said.

Once I had picked out my color, the woman waved for me to come sit in the chair next to Freeman.

"What's up, Tori?" he asked as he looked over the menu.

"What's up?" I took off my shoes and rolled up my jeans.

"I'm going to go try the paraffin pedicure today," Freeman said and handed the woman back the menu.

I sat down and put my feet in the water.

"Too hot?" the woman asked.

"No, that's fine," I said, and she handed me a menu. I looked over at Freeman. "You never cease to amaze me."

He quirked an eyebrow. "Why is that?"

"I never figured you for the pedicure type of guy."

"I know, I know. I look like one of them crusty-foot niggas." He laughed. "And you would have been right. Once upon a time."

"Spa pedicure," I said to the woman, and she got started. I caught Freeman's eye. "What happened to change that?"

"What always happens for a man to change?"

"A woman."

"It was my birthday, and the woman I was seeing at the time said that she was gonna take me out and get me something. I get all excited. I jump in her ride, and she drives me to a nail salon. I'm like, 'What we stopping here for?' She said, 'I'm gonna treat you to a manicure and a pedicure.'"

I laughed hard. "What did you say?"

"I said hell no, but I went on and did it, because she said it would mean a lot to her."

I laughed hard. "She was tired of you rubbing them crusty feet against her."

"She was smoother in her explanation, but yeah, that was the point. She told me that after I got them done. She was talking about how good they felt. I don't do the clear polish thing, but now I am a regular at these joints."

"Like I said, I never would have known."

"So, what do you think about last night?"

"What?" I leaned closer to him. "About dropping New York?"

"No," Freeman said. "About that shit with Ralph Chapman?"

"Honestly, I have no clue what was up with that."

"At first, I just thought Ralph wanted to fuck you."

"Why does it always gotta be about that?"

"Because if it ain't about money, what else it gonna be about?" Freeman asked, and I had no answer, because we were talking about men, so he was right. With men, it was always about money or pussy. "But after we actually got in there with Big Ralph, I thought it might be about something else."

"What's that?"

"Big Ralph didn't want to meet you."

"He didn't?"

"No."

"What makes you say that?"

"Because when he met you, he didn't have nothing to say to you."

"He didn't, did he?"

"No, but he kept looking at your boy Shawn." Freeman paused. "I think Shawn been talking you up to Ralph."

"'I've been hearing a lot of good things about you,'" I said, repeating what Ralph had said to me.

"Who you think he been hearing those good things from?"

"Shawn."

"You been avoiding him like you been doing Deebo?" He laughed. "'I haven't seen Marcellette to tell her it was cool.' That was bullshit, and you know it. Unless the nigga is stupid, so does he."

"So what was this about?"

"Shawn wanted you to see that he was tight with Ralph."

I thought about it. "He wanted me to see that getting with him would improve my position."

"If that's one of Ralph's boys, you'd be set. You could call your own shots."

"I'm calling my own shots now. Fuck I need him for?"

"You don't. I'm just saying that's what I think is going on."

"You're probably right," I said.

I thought that if that truly was the case, then Shawn was going to become a problem. It made me wonder if Deebo was going to become a problem too. Maybe *problem* was too strong a word. They were going to become an irritant until they figured out that I was not interested in either of them in any way and they moved on. I took a second or two to examine my choice in this matter. Not only this choice but also my choice not to fuck with men on that level and my reason why. I didn't trust men. One man had hurt me, and I directed my anger at all of them.

Deebo Burton wasn't a bad-looking man; in fact, he was actually kinda fine. So was Shawn. Getting with either one of them would be good for business, so I had to consider that. But at the same time, I knew that it would be good for business until it wasn't. The second they got tired of me or took an interest in another woman, I'd be out, and I'd have nothing but a story to tell when it was over. No, I wasn't going to let that happen to me. I was making it on my own; me and Freeman were doing just fine as partners. But he was a man too, so I needed to protect myself against him too.

Freeman and I went our separate ways after we left Gorgeous Nails. I was on my way back home, thinking about stopping at Waffle House and getting a T-bone steak and a pecan waffle to go, when my phone rang. I glanced at the display, and since I didn't recognize the number, I didn't answer. A few seconds later, I got a text message from the same number. I picked up the phone and read the text. It was from Deebo.

I wanna see you. Where you at?

"Really?" I said aloud and put the phone back in the carrier. And then the phone started ringing again. I had just silenced the phone and said out loud, "This mutha-fucka," when I heard the siren. I looked in my rearview and saw the blue lights of the Forest Park Police.

"Shit!" I said aloud and pulled over.

I got out the fake license and registration that I had paid so much money for and put my hands on the steering wheel. When the officer tapped on the window, I rolled it down, handed him my license and registration, and put my hands back on the steering wheel.

"You know why I stopped you?" the officer asked.

I smiled. "No, sir," I said respectfully.

"You didn't come to a complete stop at that stop sign because you were on your phone."

"I understand."

"I'll be right back." Time to see if the fake license and registration were worth the investment I'd made in them.

He walked back to his car and got in. Georgia had a hands-free driving law, and I was going to say that I wasn't on the phone, but then I'd thought better of it. *Don't argue, take the ticket, and go.* The longer I waited for him to come back, the more I thought about the fake driver's license I had just handed him, and hoped that it would stand up. That was when another Forest Park Police car pulled up. A female officer hopped out and talked with the first officer at his window, and then she approached my car.

"Would you mind exiting the vehicle, ma'am?" she said when she reached my open window.

"Why?"

"The officer that stopped you said that he smelled marijuana coming from the vehicle." She gave me hard look. "Would you mind exiting the vehicle, ma'am?" she repeated.

"Okay," I said and got out of the car.

"I am going to search the vehicle," she said as the other cop returned, with a ticket in hand.

I wasn't worried about the search. I wasn't riding with anything. Or so I thought until she got out of my car with a half ounce of weed in her hand.

"Look what I found under the back seat," she said, holding up the bag.

"I guess it wouldn't do me any good to say that ain't mine."

Because it wasn't. It probably was the bag that Jamarco had said he lost a month ago. But that didn't matter now.

"You're under arrest," the male cop said. "You have the right to remain silent. Anything you say can be used against you in a court of law. You have the right to an attorney and to have him present during the interrogation. If you cannot afford a lawyer, one will be appointed to you free of charge," he continued as his partner searched and then cuffed me.

Once I was booked, photographed, and fingerprinted, I was allowed to make a call. I called Connie and told her that I had been arrested and where I was.

"I'll arrange bail, and I'll be there as soon as I can get somebody to cover for me."

"Thanks, Connie. And one more thing."

"What's that?"

"I need you to call my lawyer. His name is Bryant Sheppard," I said and gave her his number.

After that, I was taken to a holding cell to await arraignment. In addition to the traffic violation, I was charged with possession of a controlled substance. When I was taken to court, I was glad to see that Shep was there and that he was talking to the people at the prosecution's table. He nodded when he saw me and kept talking. Then he came and sat down next to me.

"How are you, Tori?"

"Okay for where I am."

"Question is, do you want to go home, or do you want to go back to your cell?"

"I wanna go home."

"Good. When they call your case, you are going to plead guilty to misdemeanor possession. You'll get five years on probation, and you'll have to complete forty hours of a drug and alcohol awareness class, where you will be drug tested."

"Why I gotta do all that?"

"You had a half ounce of weed, which I told them was for personal consumption. She said, 'Drug program,'" and I said, 'Okay.'" Shep smiled. He had a nice smile, and I took a second to notice how fine he was. "Or you could, like I said, go back to your cell, wait to make bail, and we'll be back in court in a couple of months, if we're lucky. It could take longer, and you'd still end up with the same deal. At best."

"Make the deal now and get me outta here."

"Deal is made. All you gotta do now is answer one question."

"All rise," said the bailiff as the judge entered the courtroom.

We stood up.

Shep leaned over and whispered, "When the judge asks, 'How do you plea?' you say, 'Guilty.'"

Chapter 14

"Thank you for getting me out of there. I really appreciate it," I said as Shep and I walked out of the courthouse.

"Not a problem. I was glad to do it."

"What about my car?"

"It was impounded. Come on. I'll give you a ride to the
lot." Shep led me to his car.

"Thank you."

On the way there, I looked at him as he drove, and
made small talk, mostly about my case and the deal he'd
gotten me. I found myself admiring the shape of his nose,
his prominent cheekbones, and those full lips, which
were framed by the sexiest goatee, and suddenly I was
feeling him. I took a second to think if I was feeling him
or if this was just me appreciating that he had got me out
of jail. I didn't know, and at the time it didn't matter. I
continued to listen as he spoke, and I wondered if these
feelings were going anywhere and what it meant if they
didn't.

"I almost forgot to tell you. I got Blaire Elliott's business
plan back from our evaluation committee. They say that
the numbers look good and recommend that you
make the investment."

"That's awesome news. I know that Blaire is gonna be
excited."

"I'm sure. But I recommend that you don't make the
investment in one lump sum. The strategic influx of
capital at the right intervals will make all the difference

at this point." I guessed that Shep saw the dumbfounded look on my face and decided to explain. "For example, she needs to get the website up and running, so you pay for that. The next thing to put money into would be to begin her marketing piece. Therefore, while the website is in development, market research can be done. You pay for that, and the marketing plan can be developed. You see what I'm saying?"

"Yes."

"Do you really? Because how you spend your money is important."

"I understand," I said, and I understood that he was trying to protect me.

"Good. What I'd like to do is set up a vehicle that can be used to make these incremental investments that can roll into your ownership interest in the cosmetics company." He paused and then took a deep breath. "And if I've gotten the wrong impression, I apologize for saying this, but this is an investment vehicle, period. It is not a means for you to launder money," he said and then paused to get my reaction.

"You don't have the wrong impression." I nodded. "And I understand. So are you my lawyer now?"

"No. I'm a corporate lawyer, not a criminal attorney. Once I set up this investment vehicle and integrate it with Blaire's Cosmetics, the company will keep me on retainer."

I held out my hand. "Deal."

Shep shook my hand as he drove. "Deal."

After I told Blaire the news, things moved pretty quickly. Once she met with Shep and he explained to her how things were going to work, Blaire was all in. The next day, she called the woman who had given her a quote on building the website. I paid her, and she got to work on building it. And then it was on to marketing. We hired a company called Renaissance Marketing and were placed in the capable hands of one of its consultants, Derrica Chambers. Derrica needed time to come up with a marketing strategy for Blaire's Cosmetics. One week later, and two weeks earlier than expected, she called and set up a meeting.

"We need to totally redesign the packaging?" I asked after Derrica broke the news to us as we sat around a table in her office.

"Why?" Blaire asked with attitude, because this was her baby.

"Because you are marketing products to women of color that are in plain *white* containers with plain *white* labels and a fancy black font," Derrica explained.

"I see her point, Blaire," I said.

It took a while and much conversation, but Blaire finally agreed.

"With that in mind, tell me what you think of this," Derrica said, and then she showed us the marketing campaign that she had in mind and what was called a product packaging refresh. The white packaging had been replaced with red, and the product name, Blaire's Cosmetics, was stenciled on in white in the same fancy font as before, with a label on the back.

"I love it," Blaire said.

"I do too," I said.

Having approved the packaging refresh and the marketing campaign, we needed only to hand over a check.

"I know that you are working on getting your own site up and running, but I strongly suggest that you become a vendor on Amazon," Derrica said once she had the check in hand. "Think about it this way. Amazon has one hundred fifty-seven million Prime users in the US alone.

In addition to that, they have ninety-eight million mobile app users. Amazon ships more than sixty-six thousand orders per hour daily." Derrica paused to let the numbers sink in. "So, ask yourselves, is that a marketplace that you can afford not to be a part of?"

Up until a second ago, Blaire had called Amazon the evil overlord and had been totally against selling her products on the company's website. "When you put it that way, we can't afford not to be there," was the song she was singing now.

Derrica set to work implementing the marketing plan, and at the same time, the new packaging design went into production. About three months later, it was time to ramp up the product development. Up until that point, Blaire had been making all the products at her house. Originally, her plan had called for the manufacturing to be done in China or India, because they produced cosmetics products at a lower cost, thanks to access to cheaper labor and less costly raw materials.

"The downside to manufacturing in Asia is that I lose control of quality," Blaire said when she and I met to discuss how to proceed. "And the quality of my products is important to me."

"Then don't do it," I said.

"But that will substantially increase labor and production costs. And that may have the effect of restricting the products we manufacture."

"I guess it comes down to what's really important to you. The money or the quality of your products."

She laughed. "Both."

I laughed. "I hear you, but—"

"But me maintaining quality control of the manufacturing, especially in the start-up phase, is crucial to success." Blaire exhaled. "We make the products here. I'll find a small space and hire some people to do the work."

And my investment in manufacturing the products was made.

Now, all this took place over a period of about four months, and during that time Deebo had been calling me at least twice a day and sending multiple text messages, telling me about his feelings for me and what he could do to and for me. Ghetto poetry was what I'd begun calling it, because although I'd read each text and listened to every message, I had never called him back. I had set my phone so his calls automatically went to voicemail and I didn't get notified about his texts. They were just there waiting for me when I checked my messages. After four months of my ignoring him, he still hadn't taken the hint. I thought about getting a new number, but that wasn't happening.

"You know what I think you should do?" Freeman asked one day, as we sat around planning our next moves. He had a more devious than usual look on his face.

"What?"

"I think you should get close to him, so we can rob him."

"You serious?"

"Hell yeah, I'm serious!"

"I don't know, Freeman," I said.

Normally, I would be all for this, but because it would have to be me putting in the work that Kendra usually did, it didn't seem like such a good idea. But I did see his point.

"He is so into you that he will tell you everything." Freeman laughed. "I think he's a weak muthafucka and you'd be able to control him."

"I know. Don't you think I thought of all that? What a relationship with him would mean. It would be jelly, until it wasn't."

"That's why we get in, take him, kill him, and get out."

"What about Ralph?"

"What about him?"

"Suppose he comes after us?" I asked.

"Why would he? You gonna tell him that you set up Deebo to rob him and then kill him?"

"No."

"Then how is Big Ralph gonna find out?"

"I don't know, Freeman," I said, still reluctant to commit to it, because I was going to be the one that had to play nice with Deebo, and after listening to his ghetto poetry, I wasn't anxious to do the work. Honestly, I didn't know how Kendra did it.

"Just think about it, Tori. And think about how much we could get from a hit like that."

And I did. I fell silent, and I thought about how much we could get from a hit like that. Then I thought about something Freeman had said.

I think he's a weak muthafucka and you'd be able to control him.

And I had to agree. Any man who would continue to call after all this time of being ignored was a man who was willing to do anything for that woman once he got her. I knew that and had thought about it before, but that was when I was thinking about what a relationship with Deebo would look like. I still believed a relationship would end badly for me, but I wasn't thinking about a relationship now. I was thinking about setting him up and killing him. Now all the disadvantages turned into advantages.

"Okay, I'll do it," I announced, breaking my silence.

"Good. I'm tired of the muthafucka asking me why you won't answer your phone."

Chapter 15

So we were doing it.

But I still wasn't going to answer my phone. It might seem suspicious if, all of a sudden, I answered the phone and started being nice to him. What needed to happen was for him to catch me out somewhere and force himself on me, because that was the type of guy he was. Deebo was a "don't take no for an answer" type of guy. You know the type, used to getting what they want. I had busted his ego by not falling all over him, or should I say his money, the second he'd noticed me. I planned to exploit that now.

When he caught me, I planned to act mad, like I didn't wanna be bothered with him, which wouldn't be too hard, since I really didn't want to be bothered with him. But as I said, Deebo would not be able to accept that and would arrogantly proceed to force himself on me whether I liked it or not. All that would do was make him want me more. And I'd eventually relent and start acting like I was getting into him.

"I'll set it up so he runs into you somewhere," Freeman promised.

"I know the perfect place to do it," I said, and it was on from there.

As it turned out, Blaire was having a party to unveil the repackaged product line. She had rented the bonus room at the Grand Royale Events Center in Decatur. She had arranged for a caterer, hired a DJ, and planned an open bar. The event was invitation only and had a dress code.

The last thing I wanted to do was fuck up our event, so I needed a way to get him there, dressed appropriately and without his crew. That was where Marcellette came in.

I had her casually mention the event to one of his boys and reveal that I would be there. The very next night, Deebo was at Passion, looking for Marcellette. He wanted to know about the event, and she happily told him all about it right after he handed her five hundred dollars. When he told her that he was going to be there was when Marcellette told him that it was invitation only.

"So, what does that mean to me?" was what he said to her.

"Go ahead and crash. Make a scene at her girl's event and see how that works out for you," Marcellette replied.

After he thought about it, he asked her if she could get invites for him and his niggas. Marcellette told him that she might be able to get one for him, and he offered her another five hundred if she could make that happen. On the day of the event, Deebo gave her five hundred dollars, and she gave him the invitation. Then she offered him a bit of advice.

"Wear a suit."

"I don't have no fuckin' suits."

"Get one," she said and kept counting her money as she walked away.

The event went exactly as planned and was an amazing success. All the invitees seemed to love the new look of the redesigned products. Blaire had hired makeup artists and had arranged for deluxe massage chairs to be available. My plan had worked as planned as well.

I was at the bar with Connie and Marcellette when Marcellette pointed Deebo out. As she had advised him, he was wearing a suit. A few minutes later, he started making his way to the bar. My girls left me alone, and I prepared to go into my act.

"What's up, Tori?" Deebo said when he reached the bar.

At the sound of his voice, I spun around, looking as mad as I could. "What are you doing here?"

"I came to see you."

"How did you get in here?"

He reached into his jacket pocket and pulled out his invite. "I was invited."

"By who?"

"Does that really matter? I heard that you were gonna be here, and I did what I had to do to be here." Deebo leaned against the bar next to me.

"What are you drinking?" the bartender asked him.

"Tanqueray on the rocks."

"And the lady will have?"

"Stoli Elit Sea Breeze," I answered.

"Coming up."

"You look real nice tonight, Tori," Deebo said as he eyed my Kika Vargas Nono sleeveless minidress, with its sophisticated Sky Blue Tulips design. I had chosen this dress specifically for the occasion because of the plunging V-neck.

"Thank you."

My eyes and my smile may have been my best features, but my cleavage was the only thing Deebo was looking at. Instead of telling him that I was up here, I allowed him to get an eyeful.

"So this is some kind of product release party?" he asked when his gaze finally shifted to my face.

"Yes, it is. Let me show you," I said as I stood up.

I started walking away from him. He hurried to catch up.

"This is one of our products." I handed him a container of moisturizer. "The packaging has been completely redesigned, and that is what we are celebrating tonight."

"Oh, okay. So this is, like, makeup and stuff?"

"This is a cosmetics company, so yeah, like, it is makeup and stuff."

"That's pretty cool," he said as Dominique came rushing toward me exactly when I needed her to.

"Excuse me, Tori, but Blaire needs to see you in the back," she announced.

"Thank you, Dominique. Tell her that I will be there in a minute. Oh, but wait. Hold on one second, Dominique." I turned to Deebo. "Look, this night is very important to me, and I have a lot to do, so why don't you leave, and I'll call you tomorrow?"

"You really gonna call me?"

"Yes, Deebo." *I'm setting you up so I can rob you.* "I am going to call."

"Give me your word, Tori."

I raised my right hand. "You have my word. I'm gonna call you, okay?" I looked at Dominique. "Please escort Mr. Burton out," I said, and then I walked away from Deebo without another word.

I slept late that next morning and woke up hungry. It was almost lunchtime, so I called Deebo and made him bring his ass to Forest Park so he could take me to lunch. He was more than happy to and wanted my address to come and pick me up.

Not happening. You will never know where I live.

"Why don't you meet me at Everything Irie Jamaican Restaurant on Old Dixie Highway in about an hour?"

"I'll be there," he said excitedly.

That was how it went for the next couple of weeks: anytime I was hungry, I'd call Deebo and make him take me out to eat. During that time, he tried to make demands on my time and dominate me, as he had probably done with most other women.

He was an asshole.

Some women would do anything to be in my spot while he threw money at me. Every time he'd show up to feed me, Deebo always brought gifts, usually jewelry, but his favorite gift was cash. He would hand me cash and say, "Buy yourself something nice." Or "You should go shopping, pamper yourself." I imagined that was how he treated all the women he dealt with to make up for the fact that he was an arrogant, misogynistic, braggadocian asshole. But I was on a mission.

So when he said, "When you gonna let me do something other than feed you?" I said, "When you ask me."

He asked me to go somewhere, and after that, I allowed him to believe that I was getting into him. I made him feel that we had gotten close, and he began to brag to me about how he ran his business. It was all about how he was running a tighter program than me and Freeman and how I should drop Freeman and get with him. I didn't know if he knew it or not, but he had played right into my hands.

"Show me what you working with, and I'll consider it." I smiled and laughed. "You never know. It might improve your chances with me."

"How are my chances now?"

"Let me put it this way. You ain't a long shot no more. You may actually have a shot at this."

After a couple of days of telling me about it, he invited me to go around with him to all the places where he did business. The only place that he didn't take me was his stash house. He said that I was too pretty to blindfold.

"No, I'm not," I wanted to say quickly, but I didn't want to appear anxious to see his stash house. He had just unveiled his entire program to me, so I wasn't going to fuck it up. So I said, "You're right. I am much too pretty for that, and the blindfold would fuck up my hair."

He nodded and kept driving.

"Where are we going now?" I asked, because we had been to all his spots and we weren't headed in the direction of my car.

"I got one more place I wanna show you. It's my own personal chill spot," he said. "I keep a little bit of product there for emergencies."

"Like what? Somebody needs a key and can't wait?"

"Something like that."

Now I was down to go there. But then I realized that "my own personal chill spot" had to mean "This is where I take hoes to fuck." I started thinking of excuses to get him to take me back to my car. "What we going there for?"

"I want you to see it."

"Why?" I asked.

"What you mean?"

"I ain't one of your hoes, and we ain't going to fuck, so what we need to go to your fuck spot for?"

He laughed. "You tough."

"I am. And I'm not for no nonsense."

"I just wanna show you the spot, Tori, that's all."

"All right. I just ain't about no bullshit."

Deebo laughed. "I need to meet the muthafucka that hurt you, so I can kick his ass for making it hard on a nigga."

"Somebody should have kicked his ass long before he got to me," I said as we parked in front of a house in College Park.

When Deebo got out of the car, I quickly sent Freeman a text that said to call me in ten minutes, and I also sent him my location. I climbed out of the passenger seat, and as we walked toward the house, the front door opened and a man with an AK around his neck stepped out on the porch.

"'Sup, Fox?" Deebo said, and Fox nodded and held the door open for us.

When I stepped inside, there was another man, and he was armed with an AK as well. That told me what I needed to know. This wasn't just a fuck spot; there was enough product here to make this place worth robbing. Deebo showed me around the house and then led me to a room with a padlocked door. Deebo unlocked the door, and we went inside. The only thing in the room was a chest freezer, and it was padlocked too. The windows were boarded up, so there was no easy access from the outside. He opened the freezer; it was filled with kilos of cocaine. He closed the freezer and left the room without a word and led me to his chill spot, the back bedroom. And as planned, that was when Freeman called.

"I need to take this," I said after glancing at the display on my phone.

He nodded and sat down on the king-size bed.

"What's up?" I said into my phone.

"I need to see you."

"Did you get it?"

"On my way to check it out now."

"Bet. I'm on my way," I said, and then I ended the call and looked at Deebo. "I need you to take me back to my car. Now," I said. I included that last word because he was getting comfortable.

He got up and started for the bedroom door. "Are you always this demanding?"

"Yes. When it comes to business, yes," I said, stepping in front of him as we left the room.

"And when it's not about business?"

I stopped in my tracks and looked back at him. "When is it not about business?"

"You hard core, Tori, but I like it. It's what I need."

"Every strong man needs a strong woman," I said. *And she needs to be telling him what to do, or he'll fuck it up every time.*

Deebo took me back to my car, and I drove home to wait for Freeman to call me. After I sent him the text with the location, he'd gone to check out the spot. When he called, he said that everything had looked good from the outside, so what we needed to do was decide when to hit Deebo.

"As soon as possible," was my suggestion.

Two nights later, I was with Deebo, and I was acting a little friendlier than usual, so the next thing I knew, we were on our way to the chill spot, just as I had planned. Freeman, Jamarco, and Kendra were already in place and were waiting for my signal. Once we were inside the house in College Park, Deebo took me to the back bedroom, and I sent Freeman a text in code to alert him that there were five men in the house, not just the three we were expecting. Four were in the living room, and Deebo was in the back bedroom with me.

When Freeman and Jamarco kicked in the front door and shooting erupted in the front room, Deebo grabbed his gun.

"Wait here," he said and started for the bedroom door.

I took out my gun and shot him in the back, and he went down. I shot him in the back again as I passed by, and then I went to the padlocked room with the chest freezer. As the shooting continued up front, I shot the lock off the door and went in. I grabbed a gym bag off the floor, shot the lock off the freezer, and filled the bag with kilos as quickly as I could. Then I tiptoed down the hall, and when I reached the living room, I peeked around the corner and saw that two men were shooting it out with Freeman and Jamarco. I shot one in the back of his head and made my way toward the front door, with the gym bag of cocaine slung over my shoulder and my gun extended in front of me. By the time I reached the door, French had shot the one remaining man.

"Find the money!" he yelled as I left the house.

I searched for the car in which Kendra was waiting. It didn't take long me to find it, because less than a minute after I left the house, Jamarco came running out, followed by Freeman, and they dashed ahead of me and opened the back door. Before Freeman had left the house, he'd started a grease fire in the kitchen. It eventually spread throughout the house and destroyed any evidence that would lead to us.

Chapter 16

As Blaire's Cosmetics continued to grow in the Southeast region, thanks in part to our success in getting our products into a few department stores, Blaire and I began to discuss the advantages of hiring a spokesmodel. At first, I didn't see the need, but Blaire saw it another way.

"You're right. At this point, no. Hiring a spokesmodel isn't necessary. But we've got to keep our eye on the future and future growth," she told me.

"I get that."

"That means, at some point, we are looking for Blaire's Cosmetics to become a nationally recognized line, providing skin care solutions for women of color across the nation and eventually worldwide."

I nodded. "Okay. I see that. When you look at it like that, it makes perfect sense. How do we make it happen?"

Over the next month, Blaire spoke with agents and interviewed models and actresses to find someone who possessed what she called the Blaire's Cosmetics look. She settled on Sa'coya Yarrow. She was an actress who had done a couple of sitcoms a couple of years back, and she had had a small part in the hit romantic comedy *Journey to Love*. She was a familiar face, and she could speak professionally and intelligently as a spokesmodel.

"And her skin is flawless," Blaire said when she showed me her pictures.

"It is. Has she ever used the products?"

"No. But she is open to trying them. And that doesn't matter, anyway. In our original run of commercials, she is not going to be speaking."

"What will she be doing?" I wanted to know.

"The spots we're creating are meant to represent a lifestyle. So you'll see her doing stuff and flashes of the products and big-name splashes during the spots."

"How many do you have planned?"

"Two, maybe three."

It took a while to get everything together—managers, agents, film crews, a lot of shit I knew nothing about but which Blaire handled expertly. And once all that was done, Blaire planned a launch party, which was to be held in the main ballroom at the Grand Hyatt Atlanta in Buckhead.

As it turned out, the launch party was more of a press event than a party. However, there was a buffet with a Southern fare section, which was filled with pulled pork, fried chicken, collard greens, and biscuits. There was a taco bar, a Southeast Asian bites bar, an oyster bar, a pizza station, and a crackers and cheese station. There was also a light bites grill station, which featured dips, flatbreads, farm-fresh wraps, and salads. And you couldn't miss the open bar and the two-tiered cake, the individual truffles, oatmeal cookies, cupcakes, and baked cherry, pecan, pumpkin, and apple pies.

I went to the party that night with Marcellette, Kendra, and Connie, and we all ate and drank and enjoyed the presentation. Shep was there, so I introduced him to my crew.

"Ladies, this is my lawyer, Bryant Sheppard," I said. He knew Connie from my court appearance, but I introduced everybody else.

"Very nice to meet you, ladies," Shep said, and then he excused himself and moved on.

"He is fine," Kendra said and drained her glass of Hennessy Black.

"Ain't he?" Connie said. "But Tori doesn't seem the least bit interested."

"I don't want to mix business with pleasure," I said and hoped that would end the discussion.

Connie kept pushing. "But you admit it would be a pleasure, right?" Connie was the only one that knew that I hadn't been with a man since I arrived in Atlanta. And I wanted to keep it that way.

"Yes, Connie. Shep is so fine, and yes, it would be a pleasure, but like I just said, I don't want to mix business with pleasure," I said and gave her a stern look, which ended the discussion.

At the party I was introduced to Sa'coya Yarrow for the first time. She seemed to be good people, not overly impressed with herself, which was not what I had expected. I had expected her to be a diva, but she was anything but. She was cool and appreciative of the opportunity to be a part of our company and what we were doing.

By the time the clock struck 11:00 p.m., my crew was long gone, and I was just this side of drunk. That was cool, because I had booked a suite in the hotel. As I sat alone at a table and scanned the ballroom, looking for Blaire, I saw Shep again. He had been networking with the agents and managers that were there at the party, and from what I could tell, he was a little drunk now too.

"Tori!" he all but shouted when he spotted me. "I thought you were long gone." He closed the distance between us.

"Nope, still here. Owner, you know. I wanted to see everything to the end. But I'm about to get outta here after I talk to Blaire." I stood up and wobbled a bit and had to hold on to the chair to catch myself.

Shep laughed. "The moment that you realize just how fucked up you are, huh?"

"Yeah. I just need a minute and I'll be all right," I said and tried to steady myself. I saw Blaire, so I waved and motioned that I would call her tomorrow. Once she nodded, I let go of the chair and started for the ballroom exit.

Shep followed me. "I hope you're not planning on driving, are you, Tori?"

"No. I have a suite here at the hotel."

"Well, would it be all right if I escorted you to your suite? You are a little unsteady."

"Would you, please? I would hate to fall on my face. Very bad look. Owner and all, you understand."

"Of course I do," he said, and he saw me out of the ballroom and to my suite.

When we got there, I began fumbling for my key, and Shep took my clutch, dug out the key, and unlocked that door. He helped me inside the suite.

"Thank you."

Now I have to say, maybe it was the alcohol, but in the dimly lit room, Shep looked more enticing to me.

"You're welcome," he said.

I put my arms around his neck and kissed him. It was an impulse, and I had no idea how he would respond.

He closed the door behind us, pulled me closer, and took me in his arms. It didn't take long before we were both naked and heading to the bedroom in the suite. We collapsed on top of the bed. I closed my eyes and leaned back against the pillows as Shep leaned into my neck and began kissing and suckling it in spots. Then he knelt between my thighs and began sucking both nipples like they were the sweetest things his mouth had ever tasted.

I closed my eyes as his lips and tongue switched between my nipples. I kept my eyes closed as his lips then traveled down my stomach. It wasn't long before I felt his tongue circling my clit, and the sensation was amazing. Shep had my thighs pushed far apart and my feet in the air as he made circles around my clit.

With my legs in the air, I held his head in place with one hand and squeezed one of my nipples with the other. Then Shep eased two fingers in and out of my wet cunt. I squeezed my nipple harder as Shep sucked my clit and penetrated me hard with his fingers. I felt a wave rush over my entire body.

When I opened my eyes after the mind-numbing orgasm he had given me, I reached for the condom that Shep had placed on the bed earlier, and I stretched it over him before I straddled his torso and eased myself down on it. I moaned as I slid up and down his shaft, because that shit felt so fuckin' good. At one point, Shep entered me so hard that it made my pussy clench around him. As he moved in and out of me, I felt like Shep had filled every inch of this pussy that he could, but I wanted more.

He quickly spun me around, grabbed me by my hips, and entered me with one hard thrust. I bucked hard, and when Shep grabbed me by the shoulders and began to hit it as hard as he could, I screamed.

I passed out soon after, but I woke up moments later, when Shep got out of bed. Soon after that, I heard the shower in the bathroom go on. While the shower ran, I fell asleep.

Chapter 17

When I woke up the next morning, I felt wonderful. It had been almost two years since I'd been with a man, and I was happily sore in all the right places. I opened my eyes and reached for Shep, but the space next to me on the bed was empty. I lifted my head to look around the room, and that was when I saw the note on the nightstand. I picked it up and read it. It said that he had enjoyed being with me but had to rush out for an early meeting that morning.

That was all right with me, because it allowed me to avoid the uncomfortable "morning after sex" conversation, which I seriously did not want to have. But in that note, he had summed up all that I would have had to say. "I had fun, but now I gotta go."

As I sat up in bed, I saw that it was after eleven o'clock. Since I had silenced it the night before, I picked up my phone to see if I had any messages or missed calls. I did. Freeman had called several times last night and once this morning and had sent a bunch of texts. Marcellette had called to say that Freeman was at the club, looking for me. And Connie had called this morning to see if I wanted to go to a barbecue that a coworker of hers was having. I called her first.

"Hey, Tori," she said when she answered my call.

"Morning, cuz. What's up?" I said in a voice that matched my mood.

"Nothing. I just wanted to know if you wanted to go with me to an 'I'm divorced' barbecue?"

"What kind of barbecue?"

"I'm divorced." She giggled. "Two of my coworkers were going through divorces at the same time, and now that their divorces are final, they're celebrating by having an 'I'm divorced' barbecue."

"Sounds like that might be fun. What time?"

"It starts at noon."

"What time are you trying to get there?" I asked.

"About two or three . . . closer to three."

"I'll be home by then, and we can go."

"Awesome! I'll see you when you get here," Connie said, and she ended the call.

My next call was to Freeman.

"Where have you been?" he groused when he picked up on the first ring.

"I had something to handle."

"What you had to handle that you couldn't take my call?" Freeman asked, and then the answer came to him. "Oh." He paused, I guessed to allow it to sink in. "Okay, never mind. But I need to see you tonight. I'm gonna be at Jasper's gambling spot. Come by."

"I'll be there."

"Good. I need you to meet somebody, and we need to talk about that investment."

"What time you gonna be there?"

"Meet me there around midnight."

"I'll be there," I said, and then I got out of bed and headed for the shower.

When I got to the house, I called out for Connie, but I got no answer. As I walked down the hallway, I could hear that she was in the shower, so I went into my bedroom to pick out something to wear to the barbecue. I picked out a yale blue Allie Chambray minidress that I thought I would look cute in and went into the bathroom to freshen up and change.

When Connie was ready, we got in her car and proceeded to her coworker's house. We could smell the meat grilling the second that we got out of the car. It was a very nice house in Lithonia, with a big fenced-in backyard, which was filled with women and only two traumatized-looking men. As we stood in the backyard and looked around at the crowd, we couldn't help but overhear a nearby conversation.

"He ain't got no money, and he ain't ever got no money," one woman said. "So, yeah, he needed to keep it moving."

A woman wearing a royal blue blouse chimed in. "That was my first husband." She paused. "But he had other skills."

Everybody laughed.

"But after a while, even that wasn't enough to keep me from resenting him for not feeling like he needed to take on more responsibility in our marriage," she added.

And that was when I remembered that the theme of this barbecue was divorce and the celebration of it.

Another woman spoke. "My ex was an excellent provider. I had everything I wanted, and I didn't have to work if I didn't want to. But I like having my own money, so I never gave up my career."

"What do you do?" asked the woman with the blue blouse.

"I work at an accounting firm, in payables. So, like I said, money wasn't the problem. My bastard ex-husband couldn't keep his dick in his pants," she said,

It seemed that just about every woman in the yard nodded in agreement, like all of them had experienced a cheating man at least one or more times in their lives.

"Connie!" a woman cried out from over by the grill.

We headed in her direction, and she got up to greet her. "I'm glad that you could make it," she said as she smiled at us.

"Angela, this is my cousin, Tori." Connie turned to me. "This is my supervisor, Angela."

Angela and I shook hands.

"It is good to finally meet you, Tori. Connie talks about you all the time."

"Same here. She talks a lot about you too," I said, even though Connie had mentioned her only once or twice. If she talked about anybody from work, it was Andre, and she hadn't mentioned him lately.

"Help yourselves to food," Angela said, pointing. And then she led us to the table where the food was. "There is beer and a variety pack of Mike's Hard Seltzer, and there's water and sodas in the other cooler, and liquors on the table, so help yourselves," Angela said and then went back to the grill.

After filling our plates with the usual barbecue stuff—chicken, burgers, brats, potato salad, and what have you—we went and sat down to eat and listen. It didn't take long at all for me to understand why the two guys who were there looked traumatized. These women had come to the barbecue to vent about their bad relationships, and the men's wives had dragged them along, with the promise of free food and beer. After a while, one got up, went inside the house, and didn't come back. Soon the other one followed suit. I couldn't blame them. The truth was always hard to listen to.

"Lord, I hate to say it, but most, if not all, men are no good," I heard Connie say, and everybody, myself included, had to agree with her. But I had a question.

"What happened to you and Andre?"

"He is a jealous asshole. He got very possessive very quickly and wanted to control my plans, what I wore, and who I could and couldn't hang out with. Then he tried to isolate me from you, and that's where I drew the line. He had to go." Connie paused before she revealed, "I had to get a restraining order."

"Why didn't you tell me?" I exclaimed.

"Because you might have killed him," she whispered.

I started to deny that I would take it to that level, but I was lying. If she had told me, I would have got Freeman and Jamarco, and we would have hunted him down so we could talk and I could explain the error of his ways.

"I wouldn't have killed him, but we would have had to have a talk about it," I whispered back.

"And that is why I didn't tell you. I decided to let the police deal with him, and they did. Case closed. On to the next no-good man."

"For your sake, I hope there's a good man out there for you," I said. I found myself thinking about Shep and smiled over a flashback of the sex we had had the night before.

"What's up with the big smile on your face?"

"Nothing. I just got something on my mind. No biggie," I said to play it off, but Connie wasn't buying one second of what I was trying to sell her.

She started shaking her head. "Who was it?"

"Who was what?"

"It was Shep, wasn't it? I could tell by the way you look at him and how you act whenever he's around."

"First of all, he's not around that much. And how do I act?"

Connie held up her hand. "Every time I've been around you and he's been around, you act like he can have you and all he has to do is ask."

What could I say? He hadn't even had to ask, and I had found my way into his arms. I shook my head. "I asked."

"And?"

I shrugged my shoulders. "He had me."

"When? It was last night, wasn't it? I thought something was funny about your singsong voice when you called this morning."

Now it was time for me to hold up my hand to slow her down before she got started. "Before you ask fifty million questions, it was just sex. He was gone in the morning, and we haven't talked since."

"You gonna see him again?" she asked me.

"I don't know."

"Was it at least good?"

"It was very good, Connie."

"You'll see him again. Next time, he'll be the one doing the asking, and you'll be all for it, the way he got you smiling."

"Look, she's putting out the ribs," I said and got up.

Connie laughed, and then she got up too. "I'll let it go, Tori," she said, "but you know I'm right."

We got in line with everybody else, and when we reached the table, I grabbed a plate and got some ribs, wondering if she was right.

It was almost one in the morning by the time I got to Jasper Steven's gambling spot. The spot actually belonged to Ralph Chapman, but Jasper ran it for him. Although he pretty much ran everything else, from what I'd seen, Ralph Chapman didn't get his hands dirty at all. As far as the world knew, he was a promoter. Period. And he would kill anyone who said differently.

I wasn't a gambler, so I wasn't a regular there or anything close to it. Despite that, I knew a lot of the people who hung out there. Therefore, as I walked around, looking for Freeman, people kept stopping me, wanting to talk about this or that. Then there were the men that were always trying to get with me. It made me think about my night with Shep and the way he had me feeling. It caused me to look at one or two of my usual pursuers in a different light.

"Maybe someday," I told one guy, instead of saying, "Only in your dreams," my usual retort, and I kept it moving.

That was when Zaquan Butler walked up to me.

"What's up, Zaquan?"

"I think you need to go see about your boy," he said in my ear as he passed me.

"What's up with Freeman?" I asked, but he kept walking toward the exit.

I picked up my pace, walked in the direction of the main room, and got there in time to see Freeman and a man I'd never encountered before standing up at the poker table, arguing. I heard Freeman say, "Fuck that dumbass shit your dumbass is talking." He was about to sit down when the man pulled out a gun. I watched as the man raised the weapon and shot Freeman in the head.

"Muthafucka!" I shouted as I pulled out my gun. I walked toward him, shooting. I didn't know if I hit him with every shot or not, but the impact of my shots took him off his feet and he hit the floor hard.

"Muthafucka!" I shouted again. I stood over him, pulling the trigger until my gun was empty. I froze there, with my empty gun in my hand and tears streaming down my cheeks.

Jasper Stevens came up behind me and put his hands on my shoulders. "You gotta go, Tori."

Chapter 18

The Glock 19 was still in my hand, and I was still looking down at the man.

"Tori!" Jasper shouted.

I spun around and pointed the gun in his face. "What?"

"You gotta get outta here."

I looked at him and then down at the man who had killed Freeman, and I slowly lowered my gun. "Okay."

"Give me the gun and I'll get rid of it," Jasper said and reached for it.

That was enough to bring me out of my fog and back to thinking clearly. *I'll get rid of it, nigga, please.* It was more likely that he'd hand it to the cops when they arrived at the spot than get rid of it for me.

Without uttering a word, I jerked my hand away. And then I got out of there. I hopped in the car and drove away from there. I did need to get rid of the gun; that much was certain. I leaned over as I drove and got my old Glock 43 from the glove box. Once I had checked to make sure that it was loaded and one was in the chamber, I pulled into a parking lot and shut off the car.

When Freeman gave me the Glock 19, but before he taught me how to use it, he showed me how to take it apart and how to clean it. Wishing that I had some gloves, I took apart the gun and then wiped down each piece for fingerprints. Then I started up the car and drove away. I needed to get to Freeman's apartment. As I drove, I disposed of each piece by tossing it out the window into an area where high grass grew.

When I got to Freeman's apartment, I went straight for the safe. When we'd formed this partnership, I naturally had not trusted Freeman with my fifty grand, so we had bought a biometric safe and set it so that it could be opened only with my fingerprint. Then we had it built into a nightstand drawer in his bedroom. To make me feel better, the deal was that the safe would be at his apartment, but since my print was needed to open it, we would both have to be there.

I opened the safe and counted the money, and I found that instead of the hundred that I thought we had in there, there was a hundred and fifty thousand dollars. As I got something to put the money in, I laughed, because as it turned out, Freeman had obviously found a way to add his fingerprint so he could open the safe without me. I put the money in the bag, thinking that after all that we'd been through, Freeman was just another man who couldn't be trusted. As I left the apartment, I debated about giving him the benefit of the doubt and thought maybe that was what he wanted to talk about tonight.

Then I called Jamarco to find out where he was.

"Where are you?" I said when he picked up.

"At the crib with Kendra. Why? What's up?"

"There's something I need to tell you," I said, and for the first time since it had happened, I began to feel emotional.

"What's wrong, Tori?"

"I'll tell you when I see you," I said and quickly ended the call before I started to cry.

Once I had pulled myself together, I called Drac, Freeman's right hand. After he picked up, I told him what happened.

"I heard," Drac said. "What you wanna do?"

"I don't know yet. Meet me at Jamarco's apartment."

"I'll be there."

I knew how close Jamarco and Freeman were, so I wasn't looking forward to telling Jamarco and Kendra that someone had killed Freeman. "Shit, I don't even know the muthafucka I killed's name," I said aloud.

When I got to Jamarco's apartment and told him what had happened, he was mad as a hornet and demanded to know who had done it. The fact that I couldn't tell him only made him madder. When Drac arrived, he told us that the man who had killed Freeman was named Tyre Mekari.

"I know that nigga," Jamarco said. He was ready to go after Mekari's crew.

"You know what it was about?" I asked.

Drac cracked a smile. "Freeman was fuckin' his woman, Saquita."

"He murdered my boy over some pussy!" Jamarco shouted, and then he began giving Drac orders about organizing the muscle in our crew to bust back.

Drac nodded as Jamarco barked out those orders, and then he turned to me. "Is that what you wanna do, Tori?"

"Fuck you asking her for?" Jamarco shouted angrily.

"Because Tori is boss now," Drac said.

Jamarco looked shocked. I guessed Freeman had never told him that he and I were partners in this business.

"No, that is not what I want you to do. You let me deal with getting revenge on these niggas. I want you to keep doing what you're doing, and I wanna know everything that there is to know about them. Especially who moves into Mekari's position."

"I'm on it, Tori. I'll keep the paper flowing," Drac said. Then he turned to face Jamarco, nodded out of respect for his loss, and left the apartment.

"What the fuck kind of shit is this? Me and Freeman were partners long before you came along," Jamarco groused.

"That's true. You and him go back years. I understand that. The two of you came up together, but this is business."

"Fuck is that supposed to mean?"

"It means that when he needed money to expand, he didn't . . . couldn't come to you. It was me that he came to for money, and that made us partners."

"So, 'Fuck, Jamarco. He's out now.' Is that how it is?"

"No, Jamarco, that is not how it is. As far as I'm concerned, nothing has to change. I still need you to do all the things you do."

"Yeah." He dropped his head a little. "Don't think. Just do what I tell you." I'd heard Freeman tell him that on more than one occasion, and I had to agree. "I'm just the muscle. No need for me to think, right?" He shook his head. "I'm out," he said and walked toward the door.

Kendra went after him, but the next day she made an appearance without him.

"He's out," she told me.

"What about you?"

"I'm with you for whatever you need me to do, Tori. I will always be loyal to you," Kendra said, pledging her loyalty to me. "Always, no matter what."

"Thank you, Kendra."

Zakoby Means was now running Tyre Mekari's crew, and I let things sit where they were for more than a week, letting them think that we were going to let it die, call it even, or some stupid shit like that. Meanwhile, I found out all I needed to know about Means and the people around him. Once I knew what they could come back at us with, I planned to hit them hard. When me and Drac were getting ready to leave, I called Jamarco and told him what we were gonna do.

"If you really wanna get revenge for Freeman, now's the time," I said and then told him where to meet us.

"I'll meet you there."

When me, Drac, and Jamarco got there, it was like they knew we were coming, because they began firing at us through the door the second we got close. Drac kicked in the door and went in blasting. When I stepped inside, one of them fired at me. I returned fire and hit him with two shots in his chest. I looked for Jamarco; he was running up the stairs, going after one of Means's men.

I looked around and noticed that the back door was open. Then I saw Zakoby Means run out of a room. He shot at me twice and ran down the hallway. I went after him, but he was gone by the time I got to the end of the hallway. I had started back up the hall when another one of them came running out of a room. I shot him in the face, kicked his gun away, and kept moving up the hallway. I could hear shots being fired in the house. I saw Drac chasing one of Mean's men. Drac fired and hit the man in the chest. He went down.

Just then, I thought that I heard footsteps coming up behind me. I turned quickly, but the hallway was clear. I turned again and saw Means. He shot at me, and I ducked into a room, shooting back blindly. As it turned out, one of my shots was lucky; it hit him in the back before he got out the front door. I reloaded my gun and moved toward the stairs because there was still shooting going on upstairs. And then it got quiet. I stood in the living room, waiting and listening. Jamarco came running down the stairs, and then Drac appeared in the living room.

"Any left?" Jamarco said.

"I don't think so," Drac answered.

"Let's get outta here," I said, and they followed me out of the house.

Now that we had settled with Tyre Mekari's crew, I hoped that Jamarco would come back to work with me as I moved forward, but it wasn't to be. According to

Kendra, his pride was too strong for him to come back now. Although he had had no real power to speak of, he had been playing the role, and the thought of everybody learning that he was nothing but muscle was more than he was prepared to deal with.

"I went by his place, and all his shit was gone," Kendra reported, and that was that.

Chapter 19

Wow.

That is truly all I can say. I went back to my place, poured myself a drink, shot that, and poured another before I sat down. I took a minute to think about how far I'd come in the past couple of years. I had started out by slinging chicken in a small Alabama town, and look at me now.

Shit's crazy, right?

But there I was.

Freeman was dead, and Jamarco was gone. There was no telling if I would ever see him again. I took a big swallow, drained the glass, and poured another drink. I needed some air, so I went out on the balcony and sat down.

Freeman and I had been trying to build something, and now all those plans we'd made, all the things we'd talked about that we were gonna do, all of that had fallen on me now. I took a sip and wondered if I was up to it.

Didn't matter.

We were moving forward, and I was on top.

Over the next couple of months, I depended heavily on Drac, Morgan, and Dominique. Kendra was still around; she had gone straight stickup girl. If she knew you had dope or money and you were walking the street with it, you became her prey. I gotta tell you, seriously, the girl got heart.

I spent a lot of time with Blaire. Blaire's Cosmetics had taken off and was growing, and we were wisely re-investing our profits in research and development. Shep had become our lawyer—we'd put him on retainer about seven or eight months ago—and so far, it had turned out to be a good move for Blaire and me. We hadn't had sex again. It was something neither of us talked about. I went back and forth in my mind about that. But I always ended up thinking that this arrangement was for the best.

"You need to think about making some other invest-ments, other than the cosmetics company," Shep mused one day, as we all sat in a meeting room at Blaire's Cosmetics. "You too, Blaire."

"In what?" I asked.

"Real estate," Shep answered.

Blaire and I looked at each other and giggled like schoolgirls.

"Real estate. No, I can't say that I have even given real estate investing any thought," I said.

"Neither have I, I am ashamed to say," Blaire said.

"Well, you need to," Shep told us. "Mark Twain said, 'Buy land. They ain't making no more of it.'"

"Well, if Mark Twain thought it was a good idea . . . ," Blaire said sarcastically and laughed.

I gave a chuckle. "Fuck him! What you say, Shep?"

"That the current market in Atlanta is ripe with com-mercial real estate."

I grinned. "I'm in. What about you, Blaire?"

"I would need to get more information, but count me in, partner," Blaire said.

"I'll set something up with a Realtor I can trust for her discretion," Shep said and began gathering his things. "I'll be in touch with anything new. Otherwise, I will see you at our next meeting," he announced as he closed his briefcase.

"Sounds good," Blaire said.

"I'll be looking out for the Realtor," I said as he was leaving the meeting room.

I left our office feeling good about where I was and where I was going. I got in my car and drove to Passion; I wanted a drink, but what motivated me more was that I hadn't been there in more than a minute.

When I got there, Marcellette was sitting at the bar, a glass in front of her. I headed over, took a seat next her, and ordered a drink from the bartender. As I sipped, Marcellette told me about this man, a dealer from Shreveport, Louisiana, who was on her hard.

"His name is Vernon Patterson. Says he's big-time in Shreveport," Marcellette revealed.

"You believe him?"

"He talks the talk, so your guess is as good as mine. But here's the thing. He was drunk and was bragging to me about this safe he had built into the floor at his house."

"That sounds like something that has promise."

Marcellette drained her glass. "That's why I'm telling you about it."

"I'll check him out. See if he is as big-time in Shreveport as he says he is. How'd you leave it with him?"

"We're all good. He invited me to spend a weekend with him in Shreveport," Marcellette said and stood up.

"Okay. I'll check him, and if he is who he says he is, we'll take a run at him," I said, then shot my drink, and we went our separate ways.

The following morning I rolled out for Shreveport, thinking about why I was doing this. The answer was simple: I was a stickup girl at heart. The rush, the exhilaration, there was nothing in the world like it.

After I got to Shreveport and got settled at a hotel, I set out in search of our potential prey. Marcellette had told me about a few of the spots that he said he wanted to take her to after she asked him, "What the fuck is there to do in Shreveport?"

When I got to the first spot and asked if Vernon Patterson was there, the bartender pointed him out, and I began to size him up. He was exactly who he had said he was. But here's the thing: he was a loudmouthed drunk, and from the people I talked to, it made him sloppy, and the older he got, the worse it got. I left Shreveport, knowing that I had found new prey to set up and rob.

When I got back to Atlanta, I met up with Marcellette and Kendra, and they were down to do the robbery themselves.

"We don't need Jamarco and them," Kendra said and pulled out both her guns. "This one's gonna be easy."

When he called Marcellette a few days later and invited her to come down, she told him to send her a plane ticket and she would be there. It didn't take long before she had a confirmed ticket. Me and Kendra left for Shreveport right away.

By the time Marcellette stepped off the plane and he picked her up in baggage claim, we had a plan to take him. As soon as he got to the house, he gave Marcellette a tour of the interior, and he even hinted about where the safe was. All she had to do was get him fucked up and half-naked.

"Simple," Marcellette said when she called us on the sly after her house tour. We agreed on how and when she would let us know when to make our move.

When she had him exactly where we wanted him, in his underwear, fucked up, and thinking he was about to get some pussy, she texted me, and we made our move. Before me and Kendra reached the house, she unlocked the screen door in back, so that we could enter on our own and undetected.

"What the fuck! Who the fuck are you two?" Patterson screamed when I jerked a naked Marcellette out of the bed and put my gun to her head.

She began screaming, and as planned, she would not stop.

"We're party girls," I said, and Kendra pointed both her guns at him.

"Get up!" she ordered.

He put his hands up and got out of bed. He was drunk, so he stumbled when he did this.

"Shut her up!" I shouted for appearances.

"Shut her the fuck up, or I'll kill her!" Kendra shouted at Marcellette and fired one shot at the ceiling. But Marcellette kept right on screaming, and we turned our attention back to him.

"I barely know that bitch!" Patterson yelled, and Kendra hit him in the mouth with the barrel of one of her guns.

"Watch your mouth," she said and hit him again. "You will show her some respect."

"What's this about? What do you want?" he demanded to know.

"I know you got a safe here. Open it!" Kendra yelled.

"I don't know what you're talking about!"

"Bullshit!" Kendra put the barrel of one of her guns in his mouth. "Lie to me again, and she dies!"

"Go ahead and kill her. I told you I barely know her."

I fired a shot at the open doorway, and Marcellette screamed louder. "He does have a safe. He showed me where it was."

"Shut up!" he shouted, and Kendra shot him in the thigh. He screamed in pain.

"I told you about lying to me," Kendra growled. "Take me to the fucking safe and open it!"

"Fuck you! I ain't opening shit for you!" he screamed, and she shot him in the other thigh.

"Next one and you will be dickless!"

"Okay, okay!" he cried.

"Take us to the safe," Kendra said and got behind him and put her gun to his head. "Move!"

"You too," I said, pointing at a still screaming Marcellette.

Patterson made his way down the hallway, with Kendra right on his heels, to a room he used as a home office, and Marcellette followed behind him. I took up the rear.

When Patterson pointed to the place on the floor where the built-in safe was hidden, Kendra pushed him, and he dropped to his knees. "Open it!" she shouted and hit him in the back of the head.

"Okay, okay!" he shouted and began removing a floor tile to access the safe.

Marcellette quieted down while he entered the combination and opened the safe.

I wanted to say wow when I saw how much cash was in there, along with ten bricks of cocaine.

"You bitches are gonna die a slow and violent death," he promised.

Shit. I had had no idea that we would find all this. And in that second, I knew he was right. You didn't steal that much money and drugs, and nobody came looking for you. Our original plan was to let him live, but that was out.

"I'm gonna kill you before you can spend any of that money," he said as he crouched on his knees.

I hit him in the mouth and then on the side of his head. "Shut up!"

"Put some clothes on," I ordered Marcellette, and once she had her dress on, I had her pack up the contents of the safe in a bag I found in the office. Kendra had her carry the bag and walked her out of the house at gunpoint.

Once they were outside, I shot Patterson twice in the head and then put three in his chest.

I went outside. Kendra and Marcellette were already in the car. I approached and leaned in the open driver's window and said, "We can't go yet."

"Why not?" Marcellette asked and got out of the back seat.

"We need to burn this bitch to the ground," I told them.

"She's right," Kendra said and started the car. "I'll go get some gas."

Once she was back, we poured gasoline on the body and then on the house's exterior. I lit the body on fire, and we stood inside while it burned. Afterward, we got out of the house and lit it on fire. We watched it burn for a while, and then we got out of there and made our way back to Atlanta.

Chapter 20

Wow!

I know that I said it before, but damn! *Wow*, was all I kept thinking as we drove back to Atlanta in silence. I imagined that both Kendra and Marcellette were as deep in thought as I was.

"Shit!" I said aloud, finding a new word.

"I'm telling you," Kendra commented, "when you came to me with this, this was not what I was expecting."

"Neither was I, but what were you expecting?" Marcellette asked.

"A key or two, some cash," Kendra said.

I nodded. "Me too."

"What you think's gonna happen now, Tori?" Marcellette wanted to know.

"Honestly?"

"Of course."

"Like he said, you can't steal that much cash and dope, and nobody notices and comes looking for you. So, the question to you is, how much does he know about you?"

"I didn't even tell him my real name. As far as he was concerned, my name is Marvelous. He sent the ticket, and I used a fake ID to get on the plane."

"Cameras?" Kendra asked, She wanted to know, and so did I.

"I never looked at the camera. I didn't have any luggage, and I walked through baggage claim with my head down," Marcellette told us.

"Still, cops will be all over that. But we didn't give them a lot to work with," I said.

"You count it?" Kendra asked.

"No," Marcellette said.

"Do you want to count it?" Kendra asked.

"Wait until we get back home," I said, and the car returned to silence, which lasted for the rest of the eight-hour drive.

When we were back at Marcellette's house, we brought the dope and the money inside, and Kendra counted the cash.

"How much?" I asked after she laid the last bill on the kitchen table.

"I'll count it again, but it appears that there's a quarter of a million dollars here," she announced.

"What?" Marcellette said, her eyes wide.

"A quarter of a million dollars."

I shook my head. "You're bullshitting, right?"

"Count it yourself." Kendra got up from the table and went to fix a drink.

I sat down in the kitchen chair Kendra had just vacated and carefully counted the money. "Quarter of a million dollars. Pour me one."

"Me too," Marcellette chimed in.

"That's what? About eighty grand a piece," Kendra said as she poured. "I just bet you both really need a drink now."

"I didn't think it would be that much," Marcellette said.

"Nobody did," I said.

"What now?" Marcellette asked.

"We lay low," I said. "We keep as low a profile as possible. Drac, Morgan, and Dominique can handle whatever comes. But we get low and quiet."

And that was exactly what we did for the next three months. Kendra didn't rob anybody, Marcellette quit working, and not just at Passion. She quit dancing. Shit, it wasn't like she needed the money. Dancing was just a way to get spending money for her.

Me, I focused on my business with Blaire. Shep, as always, was as good as his word and introduced us to a real estate agent. She spent the next month showing us properties, residential and commercial. Some I liked and was interested in. But I was low profile and definitely not interested in making any major purchases. After a while, the agent backed off, and I told her that we would get back with her when we were ready to make a move.

During those three months, nobody came looking for us. No cops, no gangster types, nobody.

So when the three months were up, it was time for a girls' trip to celebrate. Me, Marcellette, Kendra, and Blaire went to South Beach. I even got Connie to take some time off and join us. We stayed at Shore Club, and since none of us had ever been there before, we were down to do and go anywhere that somebody said was the place to be or the place where something was happening.

"You ladies checked out this place?" was how the convo usually started.

"No, but how do we get there?" one of us always responded.

One afternoon we were out at the pool when a good-looking Hispanic man walked by where we were sitting. He passed us and then came back and stood over me.

"You're Tori Billups, right?"

"Yes," I said, horrified, and glanced at Kendra.

She nodded and put her hand on her gun.

"Do I know you?" I asked the man.

"We haven't been introduced, but the last time I was in Atlanta, somebody went out of their way to point you out."

"Do you mind if I ask who?"

"Ralph Chapman. He said that you were a very impressive woman. And it wasn't just for your formidable beauty." He had to have been at the pool party Ralph threw; it was the only time that Ralph could have pointed me out to him. "He said you were one to watch."

"And have you?"

"I know that he is, and that's enough for me."

He looked around for a server, and when he spotted one, he waved him over. "A round of drinks for the ladies." While the server took drink orders from my girls, the Hispanic man leaned closer to me. "I'm staying here at the hotel for a couple more days. I hope that we'll get a chance to talk," he said, then looked at his watch.

"I'll look forward to it," I said. "But I don't even know your name."

"Apologies. My name is Alvarez, Pablo Alvarez. And it is a pleasure to make your acquaintance, Tori."

I didn't see Pablo Alvarez again until Saturday afternoon. My girls were out shopping. I was relaxing at the poolside bar, enjoying the deep house vibes that the DJ was playing, when Alvarez sat down next to me.

"Good afternoon, Tori. I was hoping to catch you alone."

"And why is that?"

"I wanted to invite you to have dinner with me, and it might have been awkward not inviting your friends to join us."

"I see. What do you have in mind?"

"Dinner and conversation. Do you like Italian?"

"I do."

"Excellent. We'll be dining this evening at Il Pastaiolo in Miami Beach."

"Sounds good."

"If you like Italian, you'll love it there."

"I'm sure I will."

"I'll send a limousine to pick you up at seven this evening," he said, looking at his watch. "Is that a good time for you?"

"I'll be in the lobby, waiting."

"Splendid. I will see you this evening. But now I have another commitment."

"I understand."

"I look forward to dining with you. And finding out more about who Tori Billups is," he said. He stood up and waved before he walked away.

Earlier in the week, while we were shopping and I was spending money as if I had lost my mind, we were at Saks Fifth Avenue, and I dropped twenty-two hundred dollars on a Talbot Runhof two-tone sleeveless gown, though I had no idea where I would wear something like that. But this was the perfect opportunity to show it off.

At seven o'clock, I was seated in the lobby when a rather large white man walked up to me and stood over me.

"Excuse me. Are you Tori Billups?"

"Yes, I am."

"Your car is waiting," he said and extended his hand toward the door.

"Thank you," I said and stood up.

He escorted me out of the hotel and opened a door to the limo for me. I felt like I was Cinderella or some shit like that as I enjoyed the ride to the restaurant. When I arrived and went inside the restaurant, I was escorted to a table and was told that Mr. Alvarez would join me shortly.

"Thank you."

"Can I start you out with a cocktail?" my server asked when she arrived at the table.

"Yes. Bring me a mojito please," I said. I had been drinking them since I got to South Beach.

"I'll have that right out for you."

I picked up the menu, perused it, and settled on the seafood linguine. After a while, my server returned with my cocktail, and I sipped that until Alvarez arrived at seven twenty.

"Sorry I am running a little behind," he said as he took a seat.

"It's okay. I know that you are a busy man."

"But not impolite. So, I apologize for my lateness. I have to say that you look extraordinary in that dress."

"Thank you."

"Good evening, Mr. Alvarez," our server said when she arrived at the table.

"Evening, Mimi."

"Can I start you out with an appetizer this evening?"

"Yes. The Italiana cured meat and cheese board please." He looked at me. "Have you had a chance to look over the menu?"

"Yes, I have, and I'm going to have the seafood linguine."

"Excellent choice," said the server. "And for you, sir?"

"Let's try the lamb chops tonight," he said.

Once our server left us alone, Alvarez settled his gaze on me. "So, Tori Billups, tell me about yourself," he said.

"There isn't a whole lot to tell," I said and gave him my drug dealer résumé from my time with Jimmy. I talked a little about being on my own until I got with Freeman.

"My deepest and most sincere condolences for the loss of your partner."

"Thank you. Me and Freeman were going to do big things together."

"Things that I hope are still in your plans for the future?" he asked as our server returned with the cured meat and cheese board.

"Most definitely. His death was hard, but I am moving forward."

"So, you intend to move forward with Freeman's contacts?"

"Excuse me?"

"Forgive the blunt question."

"Not a problem. I have a tendency to be blunt as well."

"Good. Then we can cut out all the pretenses and speak freely."

"Please do."

"When I said that somebody went out of their way to point you out, that individual was pointing out both you and Freeman."

. I tilted my head. "Because?"

"Where you get your product is a concern to him."

"Because?"

"He can't control you in the same manner he does everything and everybody around him."

"I see. Yes, I plan to maintain and utilize those contacts. They have served us well, and I see no reason not to continue," I said, instead of telling him that we robbed that product from whoever we could, and we stole a lot from Ralph's people.

It was then that our server returned with our entrées, and that put the conversation on hold.

"Seafood linguine?"

"That's me," I said, and she placed the plate in front of me.

"And the lamb chops for the gentleman," she said, placing a plate before Alvarez. After inquiring whether we needed anything, she disappeared.

"Does that mean that you are not open to considering other options?" he asked, getting right back to business.

I shook my head. "That would be foolish of me."

"And I can see that you aren't a foolish woman."

"I couldn't be and be sharing this meal with you."

"No, you would not." His phone rang just then. "Excuse me. I have to take this."

"Do you," I said, and he got up from the table. I decided to be rude and started eating. Shit, I was hungry, and the seafood linguine looked so good. I was halfway done with the absolutely delicious seafood linguine when he returned to the table and sat down.

"Please forgive me. But a matter has come up that I must deal with. However, what I would like you to consider is allowing me to become your exclusive distributor. You buy from me, and me only. You don't have to give me your answer right now. Think about it."

"Naturally, I would need to know the particulars of that type of arrangement. But I will consider it."

"Splendid." He stood up. "I will be in touch with you in a week or so. My driver is at your disposal for the evening. And please, accept my apologies for cutting the evening short."

"Not a problem. I certainly understand that you are a busy man," I said.

He bowed gracefully and left the restaurant.

I finished my meal and ordered another cocktail and dessert before I left Il Pastaiolo.

"Where to, Ms. Billups?" my driver asked once he got in the limo.

"Give me a minute," I said, and I called Connie.

"Where have you been?" she said as soon as she picked up.

"I had a dinner meeting."

"With Mr. Alvarez?"

"Yes. What y'all into?"

"Kendra talked to somebody who said we should go to a place called Jazid."

"Well, be ready to leave when I get there. I have a limo at my disposal for the night."

"I'll let them know."

I ended the call with Connie. "Take me back to the hotel, and then we'll be going to Jazid."

We hung out there that night, and the next afternoon we checked out of the hotel and returned to Atlanta.

Chapter 21

When I got back to Atlanta, I gave serious consideration to Pablo Alvarez's offer, but I was also more interested in finding out the reason why he had made such an offer in the first place.

Why? Why me? What have I done to rate that kind of offer? I wondered.

I knew—or at least I assumed, based on the name Alvarez—that he was the son of or was related in some way to Mateo Alvarez, who I had heard was Ralph Chapman's Colombian supplier. But I couldn't be sure, and there was no way I planned to ask around to find out. All I could do at that point was to keep doing what I was doing and wait and see if I would hear from him again. It did let me know that I needed to watch Ralph Chapman, because he was seriously watching me.

That meant business as usual, and that included my legitimate business with Blaire. I still had every intention of following Shep's advice, and so I was looking into real estate opportunities again. The Realtor that he could trust for her discretion was named Brayonna Caldwell. We had gotten together, and she had shown me some properties. I'd been interested in a couple of them, but then Freeman was murdered, and then I was laying low after robbing and killing Mr. Shreveport, so I'd postponed any purchases. Now was a better, more relaxed time for me.

Brayonna showed me a multi-tenant office park unit that had 100,811 square feet of space. My thought was that if Blaire approved, we could move our manufacturing operation and storage there. At this time, they were housed in two separate spaces.

"I like it. But let me talk with my partner to see if what I'm thinking about doing is feasible," I told Brayonna as we headed to the parking lot.

"Sounds good," she said enthusiastically, and we got back in her car.

"What else you got?"

"I got something else that may or may not fit into your long-term plans. But it just came on the market, and it's an outstanding opportunity. You wanna see it?"

"I'm riding with you, so we go where you want. Besides, if it's a good opportunity, I wouldn't want to miss out. You never know, it may be just what I'm looking for."

We drove downtown, and she parked in the garage of a building. I hadn't really been paying enough attention to the building as we approached to get a good look at it.

"This whole building is for sale?"

"It is," she said.

We got out of her car and went into the building, and then we walked outside through the front doors, and I saw that it was an office building.

"Nice. How many floors does it have?" I asked as she led me back inside.

"Twenty-seven."

"Okay, you've got me interested."

"As I said, this may or may not be feasible for what you want to do. However, it would be an excellent addition to any real estate portfolio."

I didn't know if she could tell that I knew nothing about commercial real estate or that "drug dealer" was written all over my face, but as we walked through the building, Brayonna talked about things that I needed or would need to know.

"The returns for commercial real estate investment can be bigger depending on the location, market conditions, and trends, as well as the quality of the building. In this building, you'll find that the delinquency ratio computed as of the last day of each calendar month is very low as it relates to outstanding balances. As far as the occupancy rate as it relates to the property, at any given time, most of the net rentable square footage of this property is actually occupied by tenants who are paying rent or are subject to free rent for periods of ninety days or less, so the occupancy rate is high."

"I see. Then why is the owner selling?"

"He is selling off some of his properties to invest in another project," Brayonna said as we got on the elevator. "I'm sure that once your accountants and lawyers review the books, they'll tell you that for the asking price, this is a solid investment."

"I'm sure that they will." I didn't have an accountant, but I was sure that Shep could recommend one to me. The elevator doors opened.

"And this is the penthouse suite," she said with a flourish as I stepped off the elevator.

I was totally blown away by the layout of the penthouse suite. And even though the building wasn't as tall as the buildings that surrounded it, I fell in love with the view.

"The owner used the space as both office and residence." She led me into the living quarters. "It has four thousand three hundred square feet of living space. Two bedrooms and two and a half baths."

Brayonna stayed in the living room, and I walked the rest of the space alone. I was in love and had to have it.

"What do you think?" she asked when I meandered into the living room.

"I think I should make an offer and you should present it."

"Awesome. And as I said, the owner is motivated, so we can make a lowball offer and he'll take it."

"How soon can I get my accountants and lawyers in here to review the books?"

"Once I present this offer and it is accepted, right away."

"Make it happen," I said.

For the next few weeks, I was riding high on a cloud of excitement and enthusiasm as I dreamed about that penthouse suite. But as you know, all things come to an end, and real life settles back in.

"We have a serious problem, Tori," Dominique said when she caught up with me by phone, and twenty minutes later I was walking into one of the stash houses. We had been robbed, but it wasn't what I was expecting. There were three dead bodies.

"Who are they?" I asked.

"No idea," Drac said.

"Where are Hamilton and Ajax?"

"In the wind," Drac answered.

"So, what you're saying is that after they killed those three, our people saw an opportunity and bounced with the product and the money?"

"That's the only explanation I have come up with," Dominique said. "Neither is answering their phone."

"Fuck! You got any idea how long they been gone?" I asked as we left the stash house.

"I got the call about the robbery from Ajax, and then I called you," Dominique replied.

"Sounds like this was Hamilton's idea." I looked at the time. "Ain't no telling where them niggas are by now. Fuck!"

"I can't speak for Ham," Morgan said and chuckled, "but I may know where to find Ajax. But we gotta hurry."

"Let's go," I said and got in the car with Drac.

We followed Morgan and Dominique to the Millworks Apartments in Northwest Atlanta.

"There's his car," Drac said, pointing it out to me. He blocked him in the space before we got out.

"Told you," Morgan said.

"Who lives here?" I asked as we walked into the apartment building.

"Norchelle Sabella," Morgan replied.

I guessed he could tell by the look on my face as we got on the elevator that I wanted to know more than that.

"She's Ajax's woman. If he was going to go on the run, he wouldn't leave her unless he had to."

We got to the apartment and let ourselves in and sat down in the living room. I could hear Ajax in the bedroom, trying to get Norchelle to hurry up so they could get out of there.

"I'm moving as fast as I can," Norchelle shouted at him. "A little advance notice would have been nice."

"Something came up," Ajax said as he came out of the bedroom. "Shit, Tori," he said when he saw the four of us sitting in her living room.

"Going somewhere?" I asked and stood up.

Ajax grimaced. "Let me explain."

"Explain that you robbed me? Is that what you were going to explain?" I asked and took out my gun. Drac, Morgan, and Dominique already had theirs out and pointed at Ajax the moment he entered the living room.

Hearing voices, Norchelle came rushing out of the bedroom, and she immediately put her hands up.

"Where's Ham?" I growled.

"I don't—" Ajax began, and I shook my head before I shot him in the head. Norchelle screamed as his body dropped to the floor. I stood over him and put two more shots in his chest and another in his head.

As I walked toward Norchelle, she was shaking with fear. I guessed I would be shaking too. She had just watched her man die and was probably thinking that she was next.

"What's your name, honey?"

"Norchelle, Norchelle Sabella."

"That's a pretty name."

"Thank you."

"You can put your hands down."

"Thank you."

"You know who I am?" I asked, and she nodded quickly.

"You're Tori."

"So, you know your man was trying to rob me and we got a serious problem here, right?"

"I see that."

I stepped closer to her. "So, I'm gonna ask you a question."

"Okay."

"Do you wanna die tonight?"

"No, Tori, I really don't wanna die tonight."

"So, you are gonna tell me where Hamilton is and what the plan was, right?"

Once again, she shook her head quickly. "Hamilton is waiting for Ajax at the welcome center in Alabama. The plan was for them to go to Hamilton's hometown in Mississippi and set up shop."

"Thank you, Norchelle. Take care of her, Dominique," I said.

Norchelle began shaking again, and she didn't stop until she saw that Dominique was counting off money. Dominique handed her two grand.

"Somebody will be back to take care of the body and clean up," Morgan said, and then he put the barrel of his gun to her forehead. "And we were never here."

"I understand," Norchelle said, and she watched us leave, and leave her alive.

The Alabama welcome center was about a ninety-minute ride from where we were.

"When they come for the body, make sure they take the car and torch it," I said as we headed to our two cars.

"You don't wanna take it to a chop shop?" Morgan asked and took out his phone to call a cleaner.

"No. I don't trust anybody. Burn it."

Five minutes later we were on our way to Alabama, a state that I had sworn years ago I would never set foot in ever again. It would be all right, though, for two reasons. The welcome center wasn't that many miles past the state line, and I didn't think that Alabama state police would be there, waiting to arrest me for murdering the Holmes brothers. On top of that, we wouldn't be staying long. We would be there long enough to find and kill Hamilton and recover our product and money. Once that was done, we were out.

When we arrived at the welcome center, it didn't take long for us to spot his car. Not really wanting to have to shoot it out with him, in case he got stupid, Dominique got in the car with me, while Drac and Morgan approached from either side. They had their guns pointed at him, and then Dominique, who was behind the wheel, blocked him in.

"Get out, nigga!" Drac said, and with his hands up, Hamilton got out of the car.

Dominique and I hopped out of the car, and as we approached, I said, "We'll make sure the product and the money are in there. Walk him away from here."

"Move," Morgan instructed and hit Hamilton in the back of the head with his gun to get him moving.

Dominique checked the car and then opened the trunk. "I can't be sure, but it looks like it's all here."

"You head back in Hamilton's car. We're right behind you." I told her. "And do the speed limit. Understand, lead foot?"

"And you know this," she said, laughing, because she knew I was right. She loved to drive fast. She moved Drac's car out of the way, and then she got in Hamilton's car and headed back to Atlanta.

Morgan and Drac walked Hamilton to the edge of the welcome center parking lot, and once I arrived there, we headed into the woods.

When we were deep in the empty woods, I said, "Get the car, Morgan." I turned my attention to Hamilton. "Hammy, Hammy, Hammy," I said, shaking my head. "What is up with this?" I took out my gun and pointed it at his head. "I understand. You saw your chance to grab the ring and have it all," I said, pointing at him. "Look how that turned out." I shot him twice in the head, and then I stepped up and shot him twice in the chest. I caught Drac's gaze. "Let's go."

We walked out of the woods. Morgan had the car idling at the woodland edge. Drac and I got in the car, and we headed back to Atlanta.

Chapter 22

It didn't take long for word to get around about what had happened to Hamilton and Ajax, and it took even less time after that for people to start talking to Drac, Morgan, and Dominique, whomever they were closest to, and to start pointing fingers. "You know I'm straight, but . . . ," was how they always began. To me, that meant that they were tightening up their game. My take on it was that when Freeman died and Jamarco walked away, niggas thought they could do what they wanted. And if that was the case, it ended now.

Another example needed to be made.

I had been spending more time than I needed to sitting on top, playing the role, and less time in the streets, cracking the whip. Before I got with Freeman, he had muscled his way into a nightclub called Club 371 in order to run our money through. I had been there only a couple of times with Freeman, but that ended now too. A lot of the niggas who worked for me hung out there, and I was about to become a nightly fixture.

That first night when I walked in with Drac, Morgan, and Dominique, the music was blasting but then quiet set in. I could feel the eyes on us, and I could all but hear the "Fuck is she doing here?" talk in the background when Drac made some niggas get up and we took their table. One by one, niggas began to make their way to what was now my table to say what's up and to try to gauge how I was feeling about them. I spoke to some of them, but I remained stone-faced with all of them, because everybody's head was potentially on the chopping block.

But as I said, another example needed to be made, and that would be Latravis Lloyd. The real LL, as he liked to be called, was the name that had come up in every finger-pointing conversation, because he was out of control. Word was that he was Jamarco's boy, and Jamarco had let him do as he pleased because of some side deal they had made.

No problem.

One thing I knew was that the most dangerous man in the house was the man coming up behind you. His name was Malik Dixon. LL wasn't in the house that night, but Malik was, so when he came to speak with me, the reception he got was different from that of the rest.

Seated from right to left in the booth was Morgan, me, Drac on my left, and Dominique. Now, as ruthless as she was, Dominique was a bad muthafucka. Five feet, ten inches tall, cat eyes, chiseled nose, and full lips. Her tits were round, full, and she dressed to show them off. Her waist was small, and it led to her round ass. Niggas loved and hated to see her coming.

So, here was how it went. People would come up to the booth.

"What up, Tori?" they would say.

"What's up?" I'd reply, and then I'd go back to talking to either Drac or Morgan. Most of them would walk away then, and if they didn't, either Drac or Morgan would ask, "Was there something you wanted?"

"No. Just wanted to holla," most would say and move on.

But not Malik. The reception he got was different, and it did not go unnoticed.

"What up, Tori?" Malik said.

"What's up?" I replied, and then I went back to talking to Drac.

"Have a seat, Malik," Dominique said and slid over to make room for him to sit.

He looked around, smiled, because here again, Dominique was a sexy muthafucka, and then he sat down. "Thank you."

"What are you drinking?" Dominique asked him.

"Johnnie Black on the rocks," he said, with his eyes buried in her cleavage.

She signaled for a waitress. Then she turned and asked Malik, "How's it going for you?"

He hesitated before he said, "It's all been good."

When the waitress arrived, Dominique said, "Bring this man a Johnnie Black on the rocks."

While the waitress went to get his drink, Dominique made small talk with him, discussing simple shit, like his woman, anything that didn't relate to business. When he got his drink, the conversation continued until he had drained the glass.

"Well, it was good talking to you," Dominique said.

Malik got up. "Good talking to you too," he said and then walked away, looking confused, with everybody that needed to see watching.

We continued the pattern each time he was there. It was two weeks later when LL came to the club with two of his men. I could only imagine the conversations that he'd been having with Malik over the past two weeks, because it ain't just women that talk and spread gossip. Men were just as bad, if not worse. So, when he came to the table to holla, LL got treated to the same reception everybody but Malik got.

"What up, Tori?" he said. "It's been more than a minute."

"What's up?" I replied and went back to talking to Drac.

LL stood there for a second or two; then he glanced at Dominique.

"Was there something you wanted?" Morgan asked.

"No, like I said, it's been more than a minute. I just wanted to holla," LL said, and then he started to move on.

"L," I said, and he stopped. "I'll get with you later."

"I'll be waiting," he said and moved on, with all eyes on him. He took a seat at a table in the back of the club.

An hour later, I called for security and had them clear all the people out of the VIP room. Once the room was cleared, I sent Morgan to LL's table.

"Tori will see you now. In the VIP room," Morgan told him and then went back to our table.

I watched as LL and his two men got up and went to the VIP to wait. It was twenty minutes later when Dominique stood up to allow me and Drac to get up. We took our time going to the VIP; I even stopped a couple of times to holla at some people who hadn't come by the table to holla at me.

I kept LL waiting thirty minutes before Drac and I went into the room. I could see the "It's about fuckin' time" look on LL's face.

"What's up, Tori?" LL asked.

I said nothing. I pulled out my gun and shot all three of them. Twice in the chest and once in the head.

I handed my gun to Drac, and we left the room. As we walked back to the table, all eyes were on me. I had my cleaner standing by; he entered the VIP through the outer door. He took care of the bodies and sent Dominique a text when he was done. I told security that they could reopen the VIP, and we left the club shortly after that.

We were in the car, on our way to drop me at Marcellette's, when I got a call from Shameka. She was a friend of Marcellette's who used to dance at Passion. Now she was one of the women that Ralph fucked with. I paid her to keep tabs on him.

"What's up?" I said when I answered the call.

"Just thought you'd like to know that Ralph got a call and then he booked a flight to Colombia for tomorrow afternoon."

"You know what's up with that or who called?"

"No idea. I'm getting it secondhand. But I will let you know when I find out."

"Stay on that for me. Thanks."

"You know I will."

She really didn't like Ralph, but his money was right, and she enjoyed the lifestyle. But she was certainly glad to be one of many, so most nights she didn't have to be bothered with him.

Now I was wondering what had happened in Colombia for him to make that move. I hadn't heard anything from Alvarez since South Beach, when he had made me that offer. It left me to wonder what was going on, but not enough to lose sleep over. Whatever was happening down there, if it affected me and my business, I would hear about it in due time.

Chapter 23

After that, I didn't hear any more from Alvarez, so you know what that meant. It was back to business as usual. I showed Blaire the vacant space that I had looked at for us to move our operation to, and she loved it. But instead of me attempting to buy it, Blaire went to her bank and got a loan to buy the property.

"I think that's gonna be the best way to move forward," Blaire said, and I agreed. "That's gonna be our hub, hopefully for the life of the business, and you are an investor."

"More like a silent partner," I said. "But grab your purse and come on. There's something I want to show you."

"Where are we going?"

"It's a surprise."

I took her to the building that I was buying. Shep had turned me on to an accountant, and she had looked over the books. When she gave the go-ahead, I told Brayonna to move forward with the deal. The owner accepted my lowball offer, which was a combination of cash up front and a loan from a finance company.

When Blaire and I arrived at the building, we took the elevator to the penthouse. When we got off and I opened the door to the suite, I saw Blaire's eyes buck open.

"You renting this?" she asked.

"No. I own the building. And this penthouse is for me."

"You for real?"

I nodded my head and gave her the tour. "Once I saw it, I fell in love with this view and had to have it."

"This is nice."

"Let me show you the living space," I said, and the tour continued.

After the tour, I stayed in the living room and let her wander around the space, as Brayonna had done with me. When she returned, I asked, "What do you think?"

"I love it!" she exclaimed. "Office and living space." She walked to the window and looked at the view of the city. "I love it!"

"I do too," I said, and we left the suite and took the elevator down.

"I gotta say that I'm jealous of you and that view."

"Come by anytime."

"I'm sure that I will, but that doesn't make me any less jealous."

"You could always move to a high-rise in midtown."

"I could," Blaire said.

After we hopped in the car, we were quiet for the most part until I dropped her back at the warehouse.

It had been a week since I had heard from Shameka about Ralph, but that changed that night, as I was getting ready to go to the club. My phone rang, and I picked up on the second ring.

"He's back," Shameka announced.

"You know why he went down there?"

"I don't. He hasn't said anything about that, at least not to me or the women I get my info from. I just got a call from him saying that he was back and would see me soon."

"Thanks, Shameka."

"No worries. If I hear anything, you'll hear from me."

For the next week, I waited for anybody in that house to start talking about what was going on, but nobody was talking. Until I got a call from Alvarez.

"I'm going to be in Atlanta this coming Friday. I would love it if you joined me for dinner," he said.

"It would be my pleasure."

"Our last meal was interrupted, and I would relish a chance to make it up to you."

"I am looking forward to it. Give me a call when you're in town, and we'll make arrangements."

"Outstanding. I will be in touch." He ended the call, and my curiosity grew.

Had Alvarez's father died, and was that the reason that he had had to run down there abruptly? I didn't know, but I was sure that I'd find out on Friday, over dinner. On Thursday night, I got a call from Alvarez, and we made arrangements to dine at Nikolai's Roof at eight the next evening.

"I'll send a car to pick you up at seven thirty," he promised, and I gave him the address for the penthouse. I hadn't moved in yet, but I thought that it would make a strong impression when I told him over dinner that I owned the building.

On Friday evening I was dressed in an Alexander McQueen one-shoulder, bandage, cutout midi dress, the other over-the-top dress that I had bought at Saks Fifth Avenue while I was in South Beach. I had on Jimmy Choo Josefine crystal-embellished suede sandals, and I planned to carry a small Burberry TB leather convertible clutch. The outfit had cost me over ten thousand dollars, but perception was everything, and I was going to dinner to impress. I looked at myself in the full-length mirror in my walk-in closet before I left the penthouse to hang out in the lobby of my building and wait for the limo. I looked like money.

When the driver called my cell, I came right out.

"Good evening, Ms. Billups. My name is Andre, and I'll be your driver for the evening," he said and opened the door for me to get in.

"Good evening, Andre. I'm sure that I'll be in good hands."

"For sure," he said and shut the door.

Once we were on our way to the restaurant, Andre said nothing, and I looked out the window for the short ride to my destination. I was early, but I went inside Nikolai's Roof and announced myself to the maître d'.

"Tori Billups. I am meeting Pablo Alvarez."

"Good evening, Ms. Billups," he said. "I apologize that your table isn't ready yet. I invite you to wait at the bar or in the lobby until your table is ready."

"The bar is fine."

He signaled for a hostess. "Please escort our guest to the bar and open a tab on us."

"Would you mind following me?" the hostess said.

Once I was seated, the bartender headed over. "What are you drinking this evening?" he asked.

"I don't know. Surprise me."

He smiled and rushed off. When he returned moments later, he placed a drink in front of me. "French seventy-five."

I took a sip. "That's good. What's in it?"

"Gin, a dash of simple syrup, lemon juice, and champagne."

I took another sip. "I like this."

"Enjoy," he said and moved on to the next guest.

While I waited for my table to be ready, I looked around the bar and did some people watching. That was when I spotted them. Pablo Alvarez and Ralph Chapman were seated at a table near the back of the bar. And Ralph didn't look happy about what Alvarez was saying. They were deep in conversation, so I was sure that they hadn't seen me. Before I was able to finish my drink, the hostess came by.

"Ms. Billups?"

"Yes?"

"Your table is ready. Would you mind following me?"

When I stood up was when I made eye contact with Ralph. In that second, he looked surprised and then angry. I nodded and followed the hostess to the table.

"Would you care for another French seventy-five?"

"Thank you," I said as she handed me a menu.

"I'll be right back with your drink."

It was just after eight when Alvarez and Ralph left the bar. I looked on as Alvarez pointed to me and Ralph nodded. Again, Ralph didn't look happy as he followed Alvarez to the table.

"Good evening, Tori," Alvarez said.

"Good evening, Mr. Alvarez."

"Of course, you know Mr. Chapman?"

I nodded. "Of course. How are you?"

"I'm good. Surprised to see you here," Ralph replied.

"I met Tori during a recent trip to Miami. I was so enchanted that I promised that the next time I was in Atlanta, we would have dinner together," Alvarez explained.

Ralph nodded. "It was good seeing you, Tori. I'm sure I'll see you again soon."

"Once again, my apologies for being late," Alvarez said once Ralph had turned and headed to the door.

"As I said in Miami, I understand that you're a busy man."

"I promise this evening you'll have my undivided attention, and there will be no interruptions. Would you care for a drink?" he asked just as a server placed another French 75 in front of me.

"Good evening, and welcome to Nikolai's Roof," the server said. "Would you care to try one of our signature house-infused flavored vodkas?"

"I'll have a Chilcano," Alvarez told him.

"I'll see if we carry pisco. If not, can we substitute our top-shelf brandy?"

"Of course," Alvarez said. Once our server left the table, he turned to me. "Once again, I have to apologize."

I took a sip. "For?"

"For not getting back to you about the things that we discussed at our last meeting."

"No need for you to apologize."

"When I returned home, my father's condition had taken a turn for the worse."

"I'm very sorry to hear that. How is he?"

"Not good, I'm afraid. The doctors say it could be weeks instead of months."

"I'm very sorry."

"That is why it is of crucial importance that you and I solidify our business relationship," he said as our server returned to the table and placed a drink in front of him.

"Chilcano made with BarSol Pisco."

"Excellent," Alvarez exclaimed and took a sip. "Perfect. My compliments to the bartender."

"Are you ready to order?" our server asked.

"I think we are." Alvarez picked up the menu. "Do you mind if I order for us?"

"I like a man who knows what he wants and takes control," I said and wondered where that shit had come from.

He smiled, and I picked up my menu to see what he was ordering for us. "For our first course, we'll have the hamachi crudo and the beef carpaccio. For a second course . . ." He paused and looked at me. "Faroe Island salmon for the lady. And I'll have the duck breast."

"Your cheese course?"

"Sottocenere al tartufo."

"And your dessert course selection?"

"For that, I defer to the lady."

"I'll have the apple mille-feuille."

"Excellent choice, ma'am. And for the gentleman?"

"The key lime panna cotta. And can you bring us some caviar to start with, please?"

"Not a problem, sir. I will get this order in right away," the server replied and left the table.

"Now to the business at hand, while we were in Miami, I made you an offer for me to be your exclusive supplier," Alvarez said. "Have you given that any thought?"

"I have, and that arrangement would be satisfactory to me. Of course, that answer is dependent on the terms and conditions of the arrangement."

"Of course."

"But yes, I am prepared to function in that role," I said and extended my hand.

He shook my hand, and we had a deal. "Based solely on our surroundings, I think it would be more appropriate if we discussed those terms at another time."

"I agree," I said, and there was no further discussion of business for the remainder of the evening.

From there, over caviar, hamachi, carpaccio, and cocktails, we made small talk about Colombia and his family. When our server brought our entrées, our conversation lulled just a bit as we enjoyed the fabulous flavors. At the conclusion of our meal, he asked the question that I'd been waiting for since we'd met.

"Do you have any plans for the rest of the evening?"

"What did you have in mind?"

"I want to show you something."

"I'd be interested to see."

"If you don't mind, I'll ride with you to our destination." He signaled to our server. "Check please."

When we left Nikolai's Roof, he told the limo driver where to go and he got in the back with me. At that point, I had a decision to make. Alvarez was a very attractive man in all the ways that made Latin men fine as hell, but the question on my mind was, *Do I want to fuck him?* My answer was, *Not really,* but if that was what it took to make this deal happen, well, I guessed I was fucking him tonight, and I would see where it went from there.

Our driver pulled away from the curb, headed down Courtland Street, turned left onto Ellis Street, got on I-75 South, and merged onto I-20 West. When we drove past the I-285 perimeter, I began wondering where he was taking me. The driver got off at Fulton Industrial Boulevard in Mableton.

What the fuck was in Mableton at that hour of the night?

I had no idea, but I knew that I would eventually find out. The driver made a left onto Martin Luther King Jr Drive and again onto Veterans Memorial Highway, and my curiosity grew about where he was taking me, because all there was around here was industrial buildings.

"Here we are," Alvarez said as the driver parked at the gate to one of the buildings and got out. Once he had opened the gate, he got back in, drove to the building, and parked.

"Come. I'm sure you'll be interested in what I have to show you," Alvarez said as the driver came to open my door.

We walked to the building, and Alvarez used a combination and then a card key to open the door. Once inside, he led me through the building, out a back door, and over to a panel truck that was parked at the rear of the building.

He nodded. "Open it. It's yours."

"Okay." I opened the truck's back doors and found a covered pallet inside. "What's this?"

"The product I promised you."

I pulled the cover off the pallet. "How much is there?"

"One hundred kilos."

Chapter 24

"You may want to make a call."

"Right," I said, pointing at him, and then I took out my phone to call Dominique.

"What's up, Tori?"

"Where you at?" I walked a little way from the truck, but I kept an eye on it. Alvarez had walked over to an office, gone inside, and turned on the light.

"The club."

"Drac and Morgan with you?"

"Yeah. What's up?"

"I just texted Drac my location. The three of you need to meet me here as soon as you can."

"He's got the text. We're on our way."

I ended the call and went to the office where Alvarez was waiting. While I waited for my team to get there, Alvarez told me how the deal was going to work out. Then he laid out the terms and conditions of our new agreement.

"I took the liberty of making arrangements for you to fly to Cali tomorrow. Your flight departs at four forty-five in the afternoon. A car will be waiting when you arrive, and it will be at your disposal, of course. And you'll be staying at the AcquaSanta Lofts Hotel. Relax, enjoy the day, and I'll be in touch that afternoon." I nodded, and he continued. "Now that my business with you has concluded for the night, I hope that you don't mind if I take the car?"

Maybe this wasn't about sex.

"Of course not. The car is yours. My people should be here soon." And almost on cue, my phone rang. "That should be them now."

I took the call. "What's up?"

"We're in the parking lot. A man is standing at the door," Dominique said.

"Come inside, walk through the building to the back door, and go through that door." I ended the call. "That's them," I said to Alvarez.

He was already leaving the office, so I trailed behind him.

"We'll be in touch," he called over his shoulder as he headed to the back door.

When he got to the door, it opened, and Dominique walked out, followed by Drac and Morgan. Alvarez waved, stepped inside, and the door closed.

"What's up that you had us ride all the way out here?" Morgan asked.

I pointed at the panel truck and tossed him the keys to it.

Drac reached the truck first and opened the rear doors. "Whoa," was all he had to say.

"Yeah, whoa," I said.

Dominique peeked over Drac's shoulder. "How much is that?" she needed to know.

"One hundred keys," I answered.

"Whoa," she said.

I nodded. "Yeah, let's get outta here."

Morgan went to get in the truck, and I went back inside and through the building to the front with Drac and Dominique.

"What's this gonna cost us?" Dominique wanted to know as we left the building and got in the car.

Morgan followed us, and we headed back out I-20 to Atlanta. My crew listened while I told them what they needed to know about the deal and our new partnership.

I could see Dominique doing the math in that beautiful mind of hers. "We could undercut Ralph's price on every level."

"Yeah, so start putting that shit out. And make sure that niggas ain't shy about talking up the price," I said.

"I don't think you have to worry about that," Drac said, laughing.

"Seriously," Dominique agreed.

"I'm going to Colombia tomorrow afternoon," I informed them.

"You taking somebody with you?" Drac asked.

"And how long are you gonna be gone?" Dominique asked.

"I'm gonna take Morgan with me, and I don't know how long I'm gonna be gone."

"Okay," Drac said, sounding a little disappointed that I was taking Morgan instead of him. "Can you at least tell me where we're going right now?"

It was a good question. "I wasn't expecting this, or that I'd be going to Colombia, so I haven't thought about it."

"What about the club?" Dominique offered.

"The club? There's no garage there," I replied.

"There isn't, but I've seen people drive a truck in there to set up equipment and shit," she said.

I thought about it. "That could work." I looked at my watch; it was just after midnight. "What are we gonna do with it until the club closes?"

"We could close the club," Drac suggested.

I shook my head. "We're not doing that."

For a second or two, I gave serious consideration to using the parking garage at my building or the warehouse we used to manufacture, store, and ship cosmetics, but I wanted to maintain the separation of my legitimate and illegitimate businesses.

"Round up four niggas you can trust to sit outside in the truck until we close the club," I ordered.

"On it. And I'll have a spot and men to cover it by tomorrow," Dominique said.

"Get four spots," I told her.

Dominique made it happen, and when the club was cleared, the truck was driven in for the night. Drac wanted two more men to walk outside the building, and he stayed to supervise the whole thing.

"Let's go, Morgan. We've got work to put in," I said once I saw the panel truck was safe and secure, and Morgan followed me out of Club 371.

I got no sleep that night. I gotta say, that was one of the longest nights I'd spent in this business, but I'd got it done. I was able to breathe a sigh of relief when Dominique called around six in the morning and said that she had got the four secure spots I'd insisted we needed.

"I'll meet you at the club in an hour, so you can divide it up," I said to her.

"Have you slept?" she asked.

"No."

"Why don't you go get some sleep. I can handle this."

"I know you can handle it, but I can sleep on the flight."

"Then I'll see you when you get here."

It took a few hours to split up the kilos, and when everything was secure, I went home to pack some clothes for the trip. I didn't know how long I was going to be in Colombia, but I packed light just the same: one carry-on bag and my briefcase. I could always shop if I needed something. Before the clock struck 10:00 a.m., I met up with Morgan, and we spent four hours going from spot to spot, collecting cash for the kilos until we had it all. It was part of Alvarez's terms. I gave him a half million in Cali, or we had no deal, and he would send somebody, most likely his henchmen, if I couldn't raise it. All that cash went into the briefcase that was waiting next to my packed carry-on.

Drac picked Morgan and me up later in the afternoon and drove us to the airport, and we got to our gate just as they were calling for us to board the flight. Since it was such short notice, Dominique hadn't been able to get Morgan in the seat next to me or even in first class. However, once we had reached cruising altitude, Morgan offered a man in the front row five hundred dollars to switch seats with him, and the man agreed.

It was almost midnight when we landed in Cali and almost one in the morning by the time Morgan found our driver. Clutching my briefcase tightly, I told the driver to take us directly to the hotel. I wanted to change the suite to a larger one so that Morgan could stay in the suite with me, but all they had were one-bedroom suites. I tried to get a second suite for Morgan, but there wasn't even another one on the same floor my suite was on.

"We need to go somewhere else," Morgan said.

"I'll be fine for the night," I said and could only hope that I would be. Neither of us was armed, and we had a lot to protect.

"You sure?"

"Not that we got a choice. So, I'll see you in the morning," I said and closed the door.

Now that I was in the suite, I looked to see if there was a safe. There was no safe, so I went into the bathroom, locked the door, and put the briefcase on the counter. I turned on the shower, and once the water had reached the right temperature for me, I got in. The water felt good beating down on my body, and I wanted to relax and take a long shower. But my anxiety anxious about the briefcase's contents forced me to turn off the water, dry off, and grab the briefcase. I got a chair and braced it under the knob on the door to the suite and hoped it would give me some time to react if somebody tried to come in on me. Then me and the briefcase got in bed, and I was asleep before I realized it. I was awakened by Morgan knocking on the door.

"Morning," I said when I opened the door to let him in.

"Morning? You mean afternoon. It is one fifteen."

"Damn. How long you been up?"

"Long enough to shower and get dressed."

I walked back to the bed; Morgan laughed when I pulled back the covers and he saw the briefcase.

"Don't laugh." I handed the briefcase to him. "It doesn't leave your hand, much less get out of your sight."

"I got it. I should have brought some handcuffs."

"I'm going to get dressed. I'm starving. But I have to wait for a call, so I can't leave the suite. Maybe we can order room service."

While I was getting dressed, there was a knock at the door. I sent Morgan into the bedroom, and I walked up to the door and called, "Yes?"

"I have a package for Tori Billups," said a female voice.

I opened the door, and a woman handed me a padded envelope.

"Thank you." I closed the door and opened the envelope as Morgan came out of the bedroom.

"Who was that?"

"Hotel employee. She brought this." I held up a phone. "Guess that means we're not stuck in this room until he calls."

I went back into the bedroom to finish dressing, and then we left the suite and went in search of sustenance.

We ate in the hotel restaurant; the food was good, and they gave you a lot of it. While we were eating, I told Morgan, who ate while clutching the briefcase, that since I didn't know how long we would be there, I wanted to see some of Cali before the day was over.

"You wanna go sightseeing? Is that what I'm hearing?"

"You are, but no, we're not going on some tour. We have a driver, so I would be good with him just rolling around the city and pointing out shit of interest."

"I'll call him."

When the driver arrived at the hotel, Morgan and I met him in the lobby, I told him what I wanted to do. He happily agreed. AcquaSanta Lofts Hotel was located in Campestre, a neighborhood in Cali. We left the hotel, and as we cruised along, the driver pointed out the Centro Commercial Aventura Plaza, the Unicentro Shopping Mall, La Babilla Park, and Las Garzas Park before driving us to the Cristo Rey, the giant statue of Jesus that watched over Cali.

By early evening, we had driven by La Tertulia Museum, which housed a modern art collection; El Peñón, a small neighborhood with shops and a vibrant restaurant scene; and *El Gato del Rio*, the famous bronze cat sculpture by renowned Colombian artist Hernando Tejada. It was starting to get dark, and I was about to tell our driver to find us someplace to eat when the phone rang.

"This is Tori," I said when I answered the call.

"Good evening, Tori. I hope that you and your associate have enjoyed the day?" Alvarez said.

"Yes. Since I didn't want to be tied up doing something when you called, I had the driver show us some points of interest."

"I hope he took you by Cristo Rey."

"He did."

"Good. Are you ready to do business?"

"That is what I came here for."

"Have the driver take you to Pampa Malbec Restaurantes Argentinos. I will meet you there," Alvarez said and ended the call.

I told the driver where to go, and an hour later we were there. Since Morgan and I spoke no Spanish, the driver went in with us and told the hostess who I was and whom I was meeting. She picked up two menus and escorted us to a table as the driver returned to the car. Naturally, Alvarez wasn't there yet, so we sat down and waited. I was hungry and wanted to order something, but the menu was in Spanish and our hostess spoke no English, so all we could do was wait. It was an hour later when Alvarez arrived at our table. For the first time since we'd met, he wasn't alone.

"Sorry to keep you waiting," he said and sat down at the table. The two men accompanying him stood on either side of him.

"No problem." I took the briefcase from Morgan and put it on the table, and Alvarez opened it. "A half a million dollars," I announced.

"I'm sure there's no need to count it," he said.

"No. But feel free. It's all there, as promised."

"No need." Me and Alvarez shook hands. He started to get up.

"Before you go, there is one thing you can do," I said.

"Anything for my new partner." He sat back down.

"What's good to eat here? I'm starving, and no one speaks English," I said, and Alvarez laughed.

"I recommend the *bife de chorizo con pimientos asados*, which is chorizo steak with roasted peppers. And the *loma samba*. That is pork tenderloin and ripe bananas in a four-cheese sauce, with a touch of crispy bacon. You'll love it," he said. Then he called over a server and ordered for us.

"Thank you," I told him when the server walked away the table.

"How long do you plan to be in Cali?" he asked.

"With our business concluded, unless you feel the need to meet again, we'll be on the first flight in the morning."

He smiled. "That was what I expected to hear, and I took the liberty and booked your return flight."

"I expected no less. We both have businesses to run."

"I'll check to see that your meal is on its way." We shook hands again, and Alvarez stood up. "We'll be in touch."

Chapter 25

Although I had been gone only a couple of days, when I returned to Atlanta, the word was out. We were rolling with a new quality product, and the price was right. Over the next few weeks, and without much effort, my people found new customers. We even had a couple of Ralph's people sniffing around, making inquiries, but so far, they were staying loyal to Ralph.

"I think they're doing more than just asking," Drac began when I met with my crew to discuss our progress. "I think they've been buying through intermediaries."

"Through what?" Morgan questioned.

"It's called a vocabulary. Get one," Drac joked.

"It's a possibility. But it doesn't matter whether they do or not. We are going to do well, very well, with these prices," I stated.

And I was right. By the month's end, we had made more money than at any time in the past. But there was no time for me to relax and enjoy the fruits of my labor. I now had two commercial properties to manage. That meant that I had to learn how to do that, because before I signed my name on the dotted line, I had no idea what I was getting into.

It was a full-time job, but once the legit workday was over, I had the moneymaker to run. I wanted to continue to be the face of my organization, so I continued to be at 371 at night. Only now, I felt the need to be more mobile as well. I would drive by spots unannounced to see how things were running. I often was tired, and some mornings I didn't want to get up, but by that time, I was living in the penthouse, so I was just steps from my office when I rolled out of bed. I hired a receptionist, Chesiree James, who arrived daily at ten o'clock, and she didn't mind interrupting my sleep if she felt a matter was important.

I could have left the running of the building to Andrew Benjamin, who had managed the building for years, or Clinton Ackerman, who was the property manager at the property where we now operated the cosmetics business. It certainly would have been easier, but I didn't trust anybody, men in particular, so I really hadn't given myself a choice in the matter. My motto was *Learn my business, or run the risk of them robbing me blind.* Not going to happen. So it was business by day and up-and-coming queenpin by night.

At night, when it came to the moneymaking business, like I said, the word was out, and like it always did, the promise of money attracted bandits, who wanted to take what I had.

Why buy dope when you can steal it?

You know, the way I used to do it.

The four of us were out riding one night a few months after my Cali trip. Morgan was driving, Dominique was in the front seat, and me and Drac were in the back. We had just rolled around the corner near my stash house when I heard the first shot. We watched as a woman, who was driving what had to be the getaway car, moved into position in front of the house.

Dominique took out her gun. "I got the driver."

She put one in the chamber as Morgan parked on the other side of the street. Under the cover of darkness, we got out of the car and spread out as we moved toward the house. Dominique came up on the driver's side window of the getaway car and shot the driver in the head. She opened the car door, pulled her out, and shot her twice more.

"Anybody make it to the car, I got them." She knelt beside the car and leaned on the hood, with her guns pointed at the house.

"If they make it that far, somebody ain't shooting," Drac joked, but when the front door opened, he shot the first one to come out. The guy had a gym bag of my money and dope in each hand and an AK-47 around his neck. The next two came out, gym bags on their backs, and just fired away with those AKs.

We were seriously outgunned, but the four of us just kept shooting. I was able to make it to the house and get an angle on the one closest to me. I fired and hit him in the side of the head. He went down, firing wildly. I loaded my gun. Morgan and Drac lit up the third man as another man came out of the house. Morgan and Drac ducked and ran in different directions as this fourth man came off the front porch, firing a forty-five in his left hand and an AK-47 in his right. I got behind him, walked up to him, and shot him in the back of the head.

Suddenly it was quiet.

"Everybody all right?" I shouted as I stepped onto the porch.

"I'm good," Morgan said as he joined me on the porch. I saw Drac and Dominique coming toward the house.

"We're good," Dominique said.

"Get our shit. Dominique, you're with me," I said, and we went into the house. As I expected, all four of my men were dead.

"We gotta go, Tori!" Drac yelled, and once we had secured our money and dope, we drove away from the house to the sounds of police activity moving in our direction.

That was how my night went, so I slept late that next morning.

The following afternoon I was thrown for a loop when Chesiree told me that Shep was on the line. I hadn't spoken to him since I had closed the deal on the properties.

"This is Tori," I announced into the phone, glad to hear from him.

"How are you doing today, Tori?"

"Doing well. Busy as shit, but I'm handling it."

"Good to hear."

"So, to what do I owe the pleasure of your call?" I asked, and there were a few seconds of silence.

"I wanted you to know that I'm getting married this weekend," he said, and it totally blew me away. I was speechless. "I know it's short notice."

"It most certainly is," I said once I had found my voice. *Getting married? Seriously?*

You didn't think that he was saving himself for you, did you? I asked myself.

"And I'd like you to come to the wedding . . . if you're not busy."

"I have no plans."

"Great," he said and told me where and when.

I tried to act like his getting married was no big deal, but for reasons I couldn't and didn't want to explain, it was.

Getting married? Seriously?

"Got it," was all I said.

"I'll see you Saturday. Kassidy is looking forward to meeting you."

"Kassidy? Is that your soon-to-be wife?"

"Yes, it is."

I wanted to ask him, "Does the bitch you're marrying know anything about me?" but he saved me the trouble.

"You're one of my best clients." He chuckled. "So I've talked a lot about you."

"Oh," was all the response I could muster.

"So, I'll see you Saturday. Feel free to bring a plus-one," Shep said, and he ended the call.

I sat there for a second or two, holding the phone, before I returned it to its cradle. Then I sat there for I didn't know how long, trying to think about how I felt about this news. I had no claims on him. I mean, we had had sex only the one time and we had never spoken of it again. It left me to wonder if she was the reason that he had rushed out of there after he fucked the shit outta me. I was a one-night stand, and since I had said nothing about it, I was good with it, so why would he bring it up or even think twice about it?

It forced me to think about my partner, Alvarez. Despite all the sexual innuendoes that always laced his conversation, he apparently had no interest in sex with me. Not that I had a problem with that; we were in a business relationship, after all. Don't get it twisted. Since that night with Shep, I'd had meaningless sex with inconsequential and irrelevant men, but still, what did it say about me? I thought that maybe it was because I didn't present myself as a sexual being. My persona and the way I carried myself around men telegraphed, "I'm strictly business, and that is the only way to approach me."

"But isn't that how you wanted it?" I asked aloud. And I remembered saying that dick was just a weapon in men's arsenal to make me feel weak and start doing stupid shit. I was about to start tripping when the phone rang.

I picked up on the first ring. "This is Tori."

"I have Cornell Lamarck with Enterprise Recourses Management holding on line one," Chesiree said.

That stopped me from tripping, but I knew I'd get back to it.

"Put him through," I told Chesiree. After I heard a click, I said, "Cornell, how are you doing this afternoon?"

I was feeling some kind of way, so I was happy when he broke into what he wanted and talked damn near nonstop for the next fifteen minutes. The entire time he was talking, all I could think about was this wedding and a plus-one, because I was going, and I wasn't bringing Connie.

And that was when I thought about Griffin March. He was a contractor working with Blaire on the refit of the production line at the cosmetics plant. He was a good-looking man, and each time he saw me, he tossed out a compliment about how I was dressed or he made some type of flirtatious comment. To which, I would say thank you and keep it moving. He had even asked me out once, and I didn't even remember what I had told him. Griffin would do nicely for my plus-one. He had a meeting with Blaire on Wednesday, and I would see him then.

I spotted Griffin's car right away when he pulled into the parking lot on Wednesday morning. That meant that I had about fifteen minutes until he passed by my door on his way to Blaire's office. They usually had a quick meeting before they hit the floor, and they generally stayed on the floor for an hour. During my fifteen-minute window, I went to the ladies' room to touch up my hair and makeup. I was back in my office in time for him to stick his head in and find me.

"Good morning, Tori."

"Good morning, Griffin," I said. And then I asked, "How are you doing this morning?" Which was a question I'd never asked him.

He smiled and stepped in. "I'm awesome. You look very nice today." I had chosen an Altuzarra Gardner lace-up jacket that I knew he'd like.

"Thank you, Griffin. You're looking nice yourself. I like the suit."

"Thank you." He took another step. "So, when are you gonna allow me the pleasure of taking you out?" he asked, making this easier than I had thought it would be.

"I have a wedding to go to this weekend, and my date canceled. The wedding reception is being held at a fancy hotel . . ."

He smiled. "I would be more than happy to fill in," he said eagerly.

"You would? I know it's short notice."

"No, Tori, I don't mind, and it's plenty of notice. Where and when should I pick you up?"

And just that easy I had my plus-one for Shep's wedding. Once I told Griffin where to pick me up and what time, he left my office happy.

On Saturday afternoon, he picked me up in the lobby of the penthouse building, and we went to the wedding. Now that he didn't have to throw one-liners from left field at me and could sit and hold a conversation with me, I found that Griffin March wasn't such a bad guy. He was intelligent and kind of funny, he wasn't a bad dancer, and like I said, he was easy on the eyes. When it came time for him to fulfill his purpose in being there, he served that purpose admirably. It happened in the middle of the wedding reception, when Shep approached me, his new wife on his arm.

"Hey, Tori. This is my wife, Kassidy."

"It's a pleasure to finally meet you. Bryant talks about you all the time," Kassidy said.

I smiled. "It's good to meet you too." I told her. Then I turned to my plus-one. "Griffin March, my attorney Bryant Sheppard, and his new wife, Kassidy."

Griffin and Shep shook hands firmly and stared each other in the eyes.

"Good to meet you both. And I wish you years and years of happiness," Griffin said, still shaking hands with Shep.

"Thank you so much," Kassidy said before the men ended their firm handshake.

With the mission accomplished, I was able to enjoy the rest of the reception. And when the night was over, I told Griffin that I was staying at the hotel for the night.

"It would be my honor to escort you to your room," he said.

"As long as you know you're just coming to say good night, I'd like that."

He held up his hands. "I'll be the perfect gentleman."

And he was. Our night ended with a hug, a kiss on the cheek, and a promise that we would do this again.

As soon as I closed the door and stepped out of my heels, my phone rang.

"Hello."

"I need you in Cali tomorrow."

"What's wrong?"

"My father is dead," Alvarez said.

"I'll be there."

Chapter 26

Chesiree made airline and hotel reservations for three, and we arrived in Cali late that night. I left Morgan in charge of the house and brought Dominique and Drac with me. Naturally, Drac was there for security, but I brought Dominique to observe what was going on and tell me what she thought. She could see the things that I couldn't, and I had a feeling that it would be important on this trip.

The next morning, as I was getting dressed in my hotel suite, I received a message from Alvarez that the wake would begin at eleven o'clock at St. Peter the Apostle Cathedral, and that my attendance was required. Conservatively dressed in a Brunello Cucinelli virgin wool dress with monili embroidery, I entered the church at eleven o'clock sharp and was directed to where the wake was being held.

"I'm going to get in line to view the body," I whispered to Drac and Dominique.

"Want me to come with you?" Dominique asked.

"No. Find a spot where you can observe the entire room. Drac, you're with me."

The line was long, so it was fifteen minutes before I stood in front of the open casket of Mateo Emilio Luca Alvarez. Although I was raised Catholic, I wasn't a practicing Catholic, but I crossed myself, anyway, and said as much of a Hail Mary as I could remember before moving on. When I got out of line was the first time that I saw the younger Alvarez. He was holding hands with a beautiful woman with straight black hair flowing down her back, and five stair-step children followed behind them. He excused himself and came over to speak to me.

"Thank you very much for coming, Tori. It means a lot to me to have you here."

"No problem. I'm sorry about your father. My sincere condolences to you and your family."

"Thank you. It hasn't been easy, but he's in a better place now." He paused. "Come with me. There are some people I want you to meet." He led me away from his family. We went into a larger room, where funeral guests were congregating. He approached a man who was standing alone by a window.

"Tori Billups, this is Jack McQueen," he said, and I shook hands with the very tanned white man.

I smiled. "Good to meet you."

"My pleasure," Jack said.

"I need to get back. Jack, introduce Tori to some of our friends."

"It would be my honor," Jack said and looped his arm in mine. We stood in silence until Alvarez was out of sight.

Then I introduced Drac. "My associate Darios Watts, Jack McQueen."

"Good to meet you, Darios," Jack said, and they shook hands.

"Drac."

"Excuse me?"

"Call me Drac."

"Drac it is. Where you from, Tori?"

"Atlanta. And you?"

"Texas. San Antonio, Texas. But my reach extends to Houston, Dallas, Austin, Fort Worth, El Paso, Arlington, and Corpus Christi."

"That's quite an operation," I observed.

"I think so. It took me ten years, but I think I got things running just the way I need them to." He leaned close. "Should be even better now that the old man is dead."

I didn't know if I should comment, and if I did, what would I say? So, I smiled, nodded, and said, "I never met his father," and left it at that. I was glad when I caught sight of Dominique. I gave her the signal to approach.

"Jack, I want you to meet another of my associates," I said when Dominique reached us.

He smiled broadly, as men tended to do when Dominique stood in front of them, and shook her hand. "Jack McQueen, at your service."

"Dominique Pollard. Nice to meet you, Jack," she said just as a man walked by and got his attention.

"Alan!" Jack said loudly and waved. "Alan!"

The man named Alan turned and came over to where we were standing. "How's it going, Jack?" he said, and they shook hands.

"Living the dream. How's it going with you?"

Alan leaned closer to Jack. "Hoping for better things ahead now that the old man is gone."

"I hear you. Let me introduce you to somebody. Tori Billups, Alan Attmore."

"Pleasure to meet you, Tori," Alan said with what I thought was a Midwestern accent and shook my hand.

"The pleasure is mine."

Alan's eyes found Jack. "Let me holler at you for a few ticks, Jack."

"Excuse me, Tori," Jack said.

"I'm sure that our paths will cross again, Tori," Alan said, and the two walked off.

"I'm sure they will," I said, though he was out of earshot. I watched them for a moment and took note of who they stopped to talk to. "Any observations?" I asked Dominique.

"Just one, and it's only an assumption."

"What is it?"

"The people you're being introduced to are the younger, living Alvarez's people. And they are congregating on this side of the room." She cut her eyes toward the other side of the room. "Those are the old man's people."

"I see what you mean." I looked at the men and women on that side of the room. They were older, and most seemed to know each other. "That why they're mean mugging us?"

"Probably. It's a new day, and there's a new sheriff in town. Ain't no telling who else Pablo Alvarez made a sweet deal with."

"I imagine I wasn't the only one. I get the feeling that he's been putting his people in place for the future for some time now."

"Especially if he knew that his father was dying."

"I don't know that he knew he was dying, but I know he'd been sick." I eyed the buffet table and then started walking slowly in that direction. Dominique and Drac flanked me as I went.

"Patiently waiting for his sick father to die," Dominique said. "Either way, Alvarez impresses me as a man who looks to the future."

I nodded in agreement. "You seen Ralph or any of his people yet?"

"Not yet," Dominique said as we reached the buffet table and got in line.

Coffee, tea, pan dulce, which was Spanish sweet bread, *pastelitos*, which were baked turnovers, and empanadas had been set out on the table, which was elaborately decorated with candles and flowers. When our turn came, we half filled our plates. While we stood around nibbling on the bread and turnovers, other people, who I assumed were with the younger Alvarez—whom I hadn't seen since he introduced me to Jack—introduced themselves. By that time, we had been at the wake for almost two hours, and I began to wonder, since I had already paid my respects to the deceased, how much longer was I required to stay. I looked around for Jack or Alan, but they were nowhere to be found.

"Let's get outta here," I said.

The three of us were heading for the door when I saw Ralph enter the cathedral.

I stopped, and just as Ralph walked by me, I said, "What's up, Ralph?"

He rolled his eyes and kept walking without saying a word.

Drac laughed. "Rude muthafucka."

"What do you think is up with that?" I asked.

"No idea," Dominique said. "Maybe he's pissed because we're beating him on price."

"Maybe. But fuck him. He'll get over it. It's business. He's been in this game long enough to know that."

We left St. Peter the Apostle Cathedral and went back to the hotel to change clothes. The finger food hadn't cut it, and we were hungry. When we were ready, our driver took us to a place called Cantina la 15 Cali Ciudad Jardin, which I'd chosen mostly because the place had an English menu. We ordered chipotle chicken flautas as an appetizer. Drac got the wood-fired octopus, Dominique ordered the canteen chicken stuffed with spinach and cheese and wrapped in bacon, and I had pork tenderloin flambéed with El Jimador Tequila. It was good, and we left the restaurant full.

When I got back to my hotel suite, I discovered that a program that had been slid under the door. It was in Spanish, and two items were circled. One was information about the elder Alvarez's funeral service, with the word *Saturday* written below it and underlined. The other was information about an evening memorial event, with the words *Tomorrow your driver will pick you up at seven sharp* penned above it. When I called Drac and Dominique to my room to tell them about this, they got excited.

"I was hoping we wouldn't have to go to all the shit on the program," Dominique said.

"You saw the program?" I asked.

"I picked one up at the wake."

"That means we'll be here a few days longer, and so we can check out the nightlife," Drac said.

A few hours later, we headed out to sample a nightclub. Our driver recommended a nightclub called La Topa Tolondra. The atmosphere was good, and the music was hot and powerful, so we stayed until we'd all drunk more than we needed to.

At seven sharp the following evening, our driver took us to the memorial event. It was held at what I could only call a mansion. The house was huge, and it took a good ten minutes to reach it from the property's main gate. Once we passed through the front door, we were escorted into a huge banquet hall and seated. Once all the guests had arrived and were seated, several people stood up and made speeches or short toasts, none of which I understood, because they were in Spanish, but I nodded or clapped politely during each one.

When it came time for Alvarez to speak, he said something in Spanish and then added, "I'd like to thank my American friends for coming to show respect. Your loyalty to my father and this family means everything to me," before continuing in Spanish. He received a standing ovation at the end of his speech, and once he had taken his seat, staff began bringing out food and placing it on the banquet tables and pouring sangria into large goblets.

Drac leaned close to me. "Guess we serve ourselves?"

I looked around as other guests at our table began piling food on their plates. "I guess so."

While we were eating, I made eye contact with Ralph and nodded. He shook his head and looked away.

I leaned close to Dominique. "Something is definitely up with that muthafucka."

It wasn't until the meal was over and we were left to mingle that I found out what it might be. Jack told me that Ralph's shipment had been stolen after it left Jacksonville and that Alvarez had told Ralph that he still had to pay what he owed before he got any more product.

"I know he don't think we're the ones that jacked him, right?" Drac asked after Jack stepped away.

I frowned. "I doubt it. But think about the position that he must be in. Running low on product, no money to re-up, and then there's us."

"Standing by, ready to handle all that business," Dominique said.

At one o'clock the following afternoon, the funeral service for Mateo Emilio Luca Alvarez was held at St. Peter the Apostle Cathedral. The elaborately decorated church was packed with guests. It was Dominique who once again pointed out that the old man's people and the younger Alvarez's people had split up and were sitting on opposite sides of the church. I didn't know if this was intentional, but that was the way it appeared.

"El hombre virtuoso, aunque muera antes de tiempo, encontrará descanso. La duración de los días no es lo que hace que la edad sea honorable, ni el número de años la verdadera medida de la vida. Entendiendo, esto son las canas del hombre, la vida sin mancha, esta es la vejez madura. El ha buscado agradar a Dios, así que Dios lo ha amado."

The service was entirely in Spanish, so I didn't understand a word of it. I just stood and crossed myself when everybody else did. At the conclusion of the service, we returned to our hotel. We planned to catch the first flight out in the morning.

"Unless Alvarez calls me and says to stay, we're out of here," I told Drac and Dominique as we stepped into the hotel lobby.

We caught a flight at ten thirty the next morning and were back in Atlanta by eleven thirty that night. Morgan had sent a limo to the airport to pick us up.

"I got a feeling that shit is about to get off the chain in the ATL," Drac said as the limo rolled away from the airport.

"I think so too." I made myself comfortable. "We all just need to be ready for whatever happens."

Chapter 27

The night after we returned from Cali, me, Drac, Morgan, and Dominique were in the office at Club 371 when there was a knock at the door. Drac opened the door, and in stepped Kendra.

"Look what the cat left on my doorstep," Kendra said and stepped aside.

"Jamarco!" everybody but me said excitedly.

"What's up? What's up, everybody?" he said, but he was looking straight at me.

I nodded.

"Where you been all this time?" Drac asked.

"When I left here, I went to Miami, stayed down there for a while, and then I went to see some family in New Orleans."

"That's home for you, ain't it?" Dominique asked.

"It is. And it was good to be home for a minute, but it ain't home anymore, so I left there and went to Vegas."

"How was Vegas?" Morgan asked.

"Got into a few things out there. Made some money, lost some money at the tables. You know how that goes. Spent a couple of months on the coast, but none of those felt right. Like I said, none of those places felt like home. So here I am, back in the ATL."

I nodded. "So, you back now," I said and stood up. "What you looking to do?" I walked up to him. "Now that you're home."

"I don't know. I'm still figuring that out."

"But you knew enough to get with Kendra."

"Yeah." He put his arm around her.

"Like I said, I came home, and there he was," Kendra said. "I was just as shocked as you are to see him."

"I do something wrong?" Jamarco looked at Kendra. "I mean, it was cool to come through, wasn't it?" He smiled but moved his arm from around her shoulders. "I mean, it didn't seem like a problem."

From that, I figured Kendra had fucked him before she brought him to us.

"It wasn't, but this is business," Kendra said. "We in a whole new world now."

I went back to the desk and sat down. There wasn't any point in wasting time waiting for the right opportunity. There was something I needed to know, so I went straight at him. "And in that world, I really wanna know about what was going on with you and LL."

Jamarco shrugged. "What you mean?"

"I mean what kind of side deal did you have with that muthafucka to make him think that he could operate in my house with impunity?"

"What?" Jamarco asked, but I thought he knew what I was talking about.

"It's called a vocabulary," Drac said, as he always did.

"I know what it means, muthafucka," Jamarco all but shouted. "I just don't know what you're talking about. Did you ask LL?"

I shook my head slowly. "Can't. He's dead. I shot him, because he felt like he could do whatever the fuck he wanted in my house."

"Look, when me and Freeman was on top, LL was one of our heavy hitters," Jamarco remarked.

"He was. But that still don't explain no side deal."

"That's because there was no side deal, Tori. Yeah, in the early days we let him get by with a lot of shit that may have given him the wrong impression. But LL did business straight up. Maybe he got some special treatment that made him think he could get out of the box after Freeman died, but there was no side deal between me and him."

"I guess we have to take your word for it, since he's dead," Dominique spit. She had never liked or trusted Jamarco and had been glad when he left.

"So, what should we do with you?" I smiled. "Now that you're back."

"I was hoping that you could fit me in."

"You should have never left," I all but shouted. "Just when we were getting ready to build on everything I was doing with Freeman, you took your ball and ran off to Miami."

"I didn't think it was right."

"You didn't think what was right?"

"It used to be me and Freeman, and when he died, you pushed me out."

"How?"

"How what?"

"How I push you out?"

He looked at Drac. "All I'm saying is that me and Freeman went way back, long before you came along."

"Came along and bought my way in with the work I put in," I said.

"I was putting in work. Had been for years."

"But when it came time to put some money behind that work, where was you?" I paused to see if he was gonna answer. He remained silent. "You were nowhere to be found, so Freeman turned to me, and I backed the work I put in with paper. I know you ain't gonna stand there and tell me it ain't the truth." I looked at Kendra. "You preferred to throw your paper at Kendra and all the pussy you used to run after."

"You can't tell me that ain't true," Kendra said.

Jamarco looked at Kendra like he was surprised that she would say that, but I wasn't, because she had sworn her loyalty to me. "So, I'm out?" he asked.

I shook my head. "No. If you're nothing else, you're a part of this family."

"I am. Always have been. Y'all like family to me."

"And you're right. You and Freeman went back years before I came along. That is always gonna mean something."

"That's what's real."

"You're a good man to have around, and we could always use a good man with skills," I began. "But I need to know that you're loyal. Loyal to everyone in this room."

"You know that I am, Tori."

I looked at Drac. "Find something for fam to do, Drac."

Dominique shook her head.

Drac looked at Kendra. "I could put him on collecting with Kendra." He laughed. "If she'll have him."

"No worries, Drac. I got him," Kendra said.

"Collecting?" Jamarco questioned.

Drac nodded. "When bigger things come along, I'll put you in. But right now, just walking in off the street—"

"You mean that Kendra dragged him in off the street," Dominique interrupted, with so much attitude that it filled the room.

"This what I got for you," Drac added, finishing what he was saying.

"And we got work to do tonight. You can start right away and get reacquainted with some friends," Kendra said and stood up. "We out." She left the office, with Jamarco in tow.

"I hope that we don't all live to regret that," Dominique said.

I quickly turned my gaze on her. "It's your job to make sure we don't. All our jobs. Understood?"

Dominique nodded.

"Understood," Morgan said.

"Understood," Drac said.

Now that we were back and I knew that Ralph Chapman had to pay what he owed before he could get more product, we began to see the ripple effects of that. He had to be low on product, if not cash, and one by one, his people began to reach out. The first one was Shawn Michaels. Which surprised no one, since he had been trying to get with me for years. I pushed him off on Malik Dixon, who had moved comfortably into the spot vacated by the real LL.

The next one to reach out was Bowie Calbert. When Drac told me that he had approached him, I was surprised. From what Freeman had told me, he and DeAngelo Robinson were Ralph's executioners, his main guys. Did the fact that he had reached out to Drac mean that he had broken with Ralph? And then I wondered if Ralph knew about this. What surprised me more than that was when Bowie showed up at 371, wanting to talk to me.

"What does he want to talk to me about?" I asked Drac as I sat at the desk in the office.

"Says he wants to talk about Ralph and the problem he got with us."

"Show the man in."

Once Morgan had searched him and taken the five weapons he had on him, I invited him to sit down. He looked around the room at Drac, Dominique, and Morgan and then at me.

"Give us the room," I told my crew.

Once they were gone and had closed the door behind them, I said, "You wanted to talk, so let's talk. What problem Ralph got with us?"

"He thinks that you had something to do with him getting robbed coming out of Jacksonville," Bowie said as he took the seat across from mine.

"Why?"

"He thinks you're Alvarez's new favorite."

"What makes him think that, and what does it have to do with him getting robbed?"

"It started the night he saw you and Alvarez out on what he thought was just a date."

"My relationship with Alvarez is strictly business."

"He figured that out when you showed up at his daddy's funeral."

"You still haven't answered my question. What does any of this have to do with me robbing his load coming out of Jacksonville? I know there's a crew down there that runs the port. He should be looking at them."

"And he is. Truth is, he knows it was them."

"And?"

"He thinks Alvarez put the two of you together to try to push him out."

"You tell Ralph I didn't have nothing to do with jacking his load."

Bowie shook his head. "What makes you think the nigga know I'm here?"

"Truth. I thought you were buying for him."

"Not. I gotta see about my own interests. So, whether all that shit is true or not, I'm interested in this becoming an arrangement that lasts into the future."

"I believe that we can continue to find common ground."

Bowie stood up. "I thought so. And we can keep having these little chats." He smiled. "From time to time."

"I believe that would be productive too." *Especially if you can keep me up on what Ralph is thinking and doing*, I thought.

I stood up and escorted him out of the office, and my crew came back in. I told them everything he had said.

"You believe him?" Morgan asked.

"Do I believe Ralph has a problem with us? Yes. Do I believe Ralph thinks we had something to do with him getting jacked? Yes. You're gonna check Bowie out to see if the rest of the stuff he's talking about is true. See if he is really doing business without Ralph knowing," I said to Morgan.

He saluted. "On it."

"Dominique, see if he has any ties to Jacksonville. What's more likely is that he was in on that shit with them."

"Would make sense. He and DeAngelo Robinson are Ralph's security. He would know the details and be in position to let the Jacksonville people know," Dominique replied.

"They do control that port," Morgan said. "Makes sense to me."

I nodded. "Then we're in agreement. We treat the nigga like a 'disloyal to Ralph snitch.'"

The next visitor was Cash Money Carter. He had heard about Shawn and had gone to Malik for product, but he was telling the same story as Bowie. Only he was talking about Ralph wanting to sit down and talk. I didn't have any problem sitting down to work this out. But since Ralph didn't know Carter was dealing with us, he wasn't about to set up any sit-down.

"Seems like the only one still loyal to the big guy is DeAngelo Robinson," Drac said after Carter left my office.

"What about Zaquan Butler?" I asked.

"Malik got him too. Says Ralph is product and cash poor. Draining his reserves trying to cover the loss and stay in business."

I nodded. "He found a source?"

"Someone he knows in Memphis is floating him. It's just not enough to handle his people and maintain his position," Dominique reported.

"The city belongs to you, Tori," Drac announced.

It was true. Alvarez had told me that he was not going to offer Ralph the same price he gave me. Ralph was out, as far as Alvarez was concerned. That was confirmed when I got a call around four o'clock that day from my new partner. He said that he was in the city and wanted to meet right away.

"You gonna send a car for me?" I asked.

"No. I'll text you my location. Come alone."

A few minutes later I got a text with an address in Dalton, Georgia, a city ninety miles north of Atlanta, on I-75. It was over an hour's drive from the club.

I sent him a text that said, On my way.

I arrived in downtown Dalton, and the directions led me to a small coffee shop. When I went inside, much to my surprise, Alvarez was already there. He was sitting in a booth near the back. He waved when he saw me, and I made my way to the booth.

"Good evening, Tori. Please, have a seat."

"Thank you," I said and took a seat across from him.

"I'm sure you're wondering why we're meeting out here."

"No, not at all. I figure you have your reasons, as you do for everything that you do. It's not for me to question."

He pointed at the ceiling. "I like that answer. But the truth is, I didn't need, nor did I want, anybody to know I was in the state. I flew into Chattanooga, rented a car, and drove here."

"Alone?"

"Yes. I came here to tell you that I plan to take your program to the next level."

"How do you plan on doing that?" I asked him.

"I am looking for a new distributor for the Atlanta market."

"From what I can tell, you've already done that."

"No. This is just a setback for Ralph. I've seen him come back from worse situations, and he'll recover and regroup from this."

"So, what are you prepared to do to take my program to the next level?"

He wagged a finger. "It's not what I'm prepared to do. It is what you're prepared to do to reach the next level."

"I'm listening."

"Eliminate Ralph Chapman, and the state, not just the Atlanta market, are yours."

Chapter 28

"Hello," I said into my phone.

"Where are you?" Chesiree asked frantically.

"What's wrong?"

"You're ten o'clock, Simon Riddley, with Sheridan Power, is here, and you're not."

"Shit." I sat up in bed. "Apologize for me and see if we can reschedule until this afternoon?"

"Hold on," Chesiree said, and I was treated to my light jazz hold music. I had no excuse; I had just overslept. After I met with Alvarez, I had gone to the club, and since her place was closer, I had crashed at Marcellette's. Had I gone home, Chesiree would have woken me up early, and this wouldn't be a problem.

"Tori?"

"I'm here."

"He said this afternoon doesn't work for him. And he'll be out of town until next week."

"Fuck."

"I made him another appointment for next Tuesday."

"Thank you, Chesiree."

"Are you coming in today?"

"Yes. I'll be there in an hour and a half."

"I'll push back your other appointments. Do you want me to forward your calls?"

"I'll let you know," I said, then ended the call and rolled out of bed.

This wasn't the first meeting I'd missed. My last-minute trips to Cali over the past few weeks were the cause for my other missed meetings. The truth was that I had too much going on, and I needed more help. I needed to hire somebody, but it had to be somebody I trusted. I could think of only one person. She had experience in management, and now that experience included the management of multiple properties. And more importantly, I knew I could trust her.

I knew that she didn't want any part of the drug business or that money. But this side of my business was legitimate. No reason I should be making all this money and she would not be down.

"I need you," I said, cutting right to the chase, after we sat down at a table in her favorite coffee shop. I had invited her to meet me there to discuss an important matter.

"Why me?" Connie asked. "I don't know anything about property management."

"Because you do know how to manage, and you can learn property management. I didn't know shit about it either. I learned, and if I can, I know that you can, Connie. Come on, say yes. I need you."

"I don't know, Tori," Connie said.

I smiled. "You'll do it," I declared.

She smiled. "How you know I'll do it?"

"Because I need you to. That, and I'll pay you four times what you're making now."

Both of us smiled. "You're right," she said. "But it's not about the money."

"Of course not."

"Your family and you need me. I can make the sacrifice for family, and four times what I make now ain't a bad thing."

I didn't know why I hadn't done this sooner. Whether I needed her or not, Connie was family. But now that she was on board, I could focus on the major issue at hand, the elimination of Ralph Chapman. I had no idea how I was going to get it done, and once I did, what would come next. Then something unexpected happened.

Now, I'll be honest with you. I hate fake phony people. They get on my nerves. And that was Kishana Tirrell. Everything about her was fake. Fake hair, fake nails, fake eyes, fake tits, implants in her ass. She had even had one of her ribs removed so her waist would look smaller. That ain't even her real name. Her real name was Kathy Johnson. She was one of Ralph Chapman's women. What was unexpected was that she and two of his people walked into the club.

"What is she doing here?" Morgan asked when her presence was brought to our attention.

"Maybe she's here to do business like the rest of them?" Drac said.

"I don't think so," Dominique said. "As far as I know, she's not involved in the business."

"I know. Maybe she's here for Ralph," Drac said.

"Or maybe she just came here to hang out," I said. "But I doubt it."

"Observation?" Dominique questioned.

"That's more likely than thinking she's here to do business," I said.

Kishana had been in our house for over an hour when she reached out and said that she wanted to talk.

"Show the lady in, Drac," I said. "And everybody play nice."

Five minutes later Drac led Kishana into the office, and after we got done with the pleasantries, I found out why she was there.

"I'm not going to waste any of your time, Tori, so I'll get right to it," she said after she took a seat across from me at my desk.

"I appreciate it."

"Ralph wants to have a meeting with you."

"What does Ralph want to talk about?"

Kishana shrugged. "He didn't say what he wanted to talk about."

"When and where does he want the meeting to take place?"

"This Saturday night at his place."

"Saturday is cool, but it ain't happening at his place. It needs to be at a neutral location."

Kishana stood up. "I'll pass that on to Ralph and get back to you with a location."

"That's fine. I look forward to hearing from you. Drac, please escort our guest out."

"What's up with that?" Morgan asked as soon as the door closed.

"I don't know," I said.

"You trust her?" Dominique asked.

"Oh, hell no," I said, thinking that this did present me with an opportunity. I hadn't told my crew that Alvarez wanted me to kill Ralph. "But I'm thinking that he wants to talk about us taking his business."

"I think it's deeper than that, Tori," Dominique said.

I leaned back in my chair. "I'm listening."

"I don't know, but I think he wants to do more than talk."

"I agree," Morgan interjected. "We should tell the muthafucka to kiss your ass."

"Let's see where he wants to meet first, and then I'll decide if sitting down with him is in our best interest," I said, but I had something more in mind for Mr. Ralph Chapman. I just wasn't ready to share.

***

It was Thursday night when Kishana sent word that Ralph wanted to meet at a closed restaurant called Journey. It used to be the hot spot, until the owners got arrested by the FBI on fraud charges.

"I know the place," Morgan commented as we sat around the office at the club.

"All the same, I wanna roll by there and check it out," I said and picked up the phone. I dialed Kendra.

"What's up?" Kendra asked when she picked up.

"I need to see you and Jamarco tonight."

"I'll round him up and come by the club."

I thought about it. "No. Meet me at the penthouse."

"We'll be there."

I stood up. "Dominique, you're with me."

Dominique and I left the club in a hurry, and she drove us to my building. I had been at the penthouse for a half hour when Kendra and Jamarco got there. Since it was their first time there, I showed them around before I told them what I had in mind.

"I plan to kill Ralph Chapman." There was silence in the room. "Ain't nobody got nothing to say?"

"Killing Ralph?" Jamarco questioned. "That's a tall order."

"But not impossible," Kendra added.

"Ralph wants to have a sit-down with me at a closed restaurant called Journey on Saturday night. At that meeting, I plan to kill him." Once again, there was silence in the room. "You two in?"

Kendra and Jamarco looked at each other.

"I'm in," Kendra said and smiled, because she was always down for whatever I needed. "But you already knew I would be."

"I never liked the muthafucka no way," Jamarco said. "It gonna be more than just the four of us?"

"Yes," I said and told them my plan.

Once that was done, I sent word to Ralph that the location was acceptable, but I would meet only if it was just us and two of our people. He sent word back that the terms were acceptable to him, and the meeting was set. Now that it was on, I summoned Drac and Morgan to the penthouse and filled them in on what I had planned as soon as they came through the penthouse door.

"No problem," Drac said.

"The nigga's gonna die Saturday night," Morgan said.

"So, what are the exact details of this plan?" Dominique asked, and I laid it all out for them.

When we got to Journey, the plan was for me, Morgan, and Drac to go in, and once we were inside, Kendra and Jamarco would come in, masked, ten minutes after that and start blasting. Dominique would drive up ten minutes later and wait outside, in case we needed her to assist. But when we rolled up to the restaurant on Saturday night, we discovered that Ralph had two people posted outside. I called Jamarco, who was riding with Kendra.

"No worries, Tori. We'll hit them first, and then we'll go inside."

When me, Morgan, and Drac got out of the car, I complained to Ralph's people that their being outside wasn't what we had agreed to. Then I went inside the restaurant with my people. But once we were inside, we discovered there was nobody in there. And then I saw somebody step out with a gun.

"It's a trap!" I shouted.

Two men stood up from behind the bar and started shooting, and we ran for cover. Two more men seemed to appear out of nowhere and sprayed the room with bullets. I crawled along the floor, trying to make it to a spot where I could get a clear shot at Ralph's men. When one stopped to reload a fresh clip, Drac stood up and hit him with two shots to the chest. The man went down, and Drac took cover as the man's partner began firing at him. With his attention diverted, I shot the man in the back.

The other two gunmen continued firing, and Drac and Morgan returned their fire. I stayed low and made my way toward the bar for cover, firing shots along the way. I reloaded my gun, flipped over a table for cover, and fired back. I hit one of the gunmen with three shots. That was when I saw Ralph. He opened fire at me, and we exchanged shots.

Ralph's men blanketed the place with bullets. One fired and hit Morgan with two shots, but Morgan kept firing at the man until he killed him. The gun slipped from his hand, and he fell to the floor. When the other gunman stood up, Drac fired twice and hit him with one to the chest and one to the head.

Ralph and I exchanged shots until his gun was empty. He ran toward the back of the restaurant, then ducked into the kitchen, and I went after him. This gave him plenty of time to reload. As soon as I came through the door, shots whizzed by me, and I had to dive for the floor and crawl to cover. He fired shots at me until once again, his gun was empty.

"Got him now." I stood up, smiling, since he had left his right side open in order to fire at me. Aiming my gun at him, I growled, "Die, muthafucka." I pulled the trigger. "Oh, shit," I said, because my gun was empty too.

Now it was Ralph who was smiling. "You're gonna die now, bitch," he said, running toward me.

I threw my gun at him and tried to run, but I didn't get far before he grabbed me by the hair and pulled me to the floor. He picked me up by the arm and punched me in the face. I went down and tried to crawl away, but he grabbed me again. I began hitting him as hard as I could in his chest; it was like he didn't even feel it. He punched me so hard, it knocked me off my feet, and I landed hard on the floor. I tried to crawl away again, but he picked me up and began choking me.

"Now you die," he snarled.

I punched and kicked him with everything I had, but all it did was make my hands hurt. That was when I heard the shot, and he suddenly loosened his grip. When he let go of me and turned, I saw Kendra standing there. He ran at her, and she fired shots at him until her gun was empty and he went down hard.

"You all right?" she asked and reloaded her gun.

I grabbed it out of her hand and stood over Ralph and shot him in the head. "I am now."

Chapter 29

Ralph Chapman was dead. But I needed Alvarez and everybody else to know who had done the deadly deed.

"Take a picture, Kendra," I said as Jamarco came into the kitchen.

"We need to get outta here, Tori," he said.

"One second." I knelt next to Ralph's body, and Kendra took the picture. "I need proof of the kill."

"For who?" Jamarco asked and then followed me and Kendra out of the kitchen.

Drac was holding Morgan. He had taken a couple of shots during the firefight.

"How's he?" I asked, barely masking my concern.

"I can make it," Morgan said and struggled to get to his feet. He put one arm around Drac's shoulder and the other around Jamarco's, and we headed out of the restaurant. Dominique was waiting for us outside.

"Oh shit!" she said when she saw Morgan. "What happened?"

"Soldier took two for the cause," Drac said.

Dominique stepped closer to Morgan to lend a hand. "You all right?"

"I'm okay," Morgan said, and then we put him in Dominique's car.

I leaned close to her as she went to get behind the wheel. "It's bad. He needs a doctor."

"He can't go to a hospital," she told me.

"I know somebody," Jamarco said. "She's only a nurse, but she's close by."

"Go with them," I said, and Jamarco got in the car with Dominique. "Kendra, you drive alone. And follow us."

Kendra climbed in her car, turned on the engine, and waited.

"We need to get outta here, Tori," Drac said as the sounds of police activity got louder. "Cops will be here soon."

"Guess we don't have time to move these bodies inside and set the joint on fire," I said, walking quickly to the car.

Drac shook his head. "Not unless you want to see the inside of a police car."

"Not tonight." I got in the car, and Drac slipped into the driver's seat. "Follow Dominique."

We followed Dominique to Jamarco's nurse friend's apartment. She was understandably reluctant to get involved at first. I couldn't tell you if it was the money I offered or Dominique putting a gun to her head and swearing to kill her, but she had a change of heart. She did the best she could and removed the bullets, but despite that, Morgan died minutes later from those two shots. I had to wrestle the gun away from Dominique, and Drac had to carry her out as she screamed, "I'll kill you for letting him die."

"I'm sorry. I did the best I could, but he really needed to go to the hospital," the nurse said, hoping that she'd live through the night.

"It's all right," I said and put Dominique's gun away. "You did your best." I put my gun in her face. "We were never here, and you never treated him. Understand?"

She shook her head vigorously. "I understand."

"Clean up and let's get outta here," I said to Jamarco, and once he had helped her clean up, we took the body and left.

"What are we going to do with his body?" Kendra asked on the way to our cars.

"I was gonna ask about the guy you know that works at the mortuary, but we've involved too many outsiders already," I said.

"He's shaky, anyway. Cops lean too hard on him, he'd give them everything he knows," Kendra said, shaking her head. "Best we bury him ourselves tonight."

"You know a spot?"

"I was thinking about driving out to the country," she replied.

"If you got a spot, tell Drac to follow you there."

"What about Dominique?" Kendra asked, because she was taking it hard.

I looked over at her sitting in the car, with her head buried in the palms of her hands. When she looked up, I saw that her tears had stained her makeup. "I'll talk to her."

Once Dominique assured me that she was going to be all right, we took our fallen soldier out to Brooks, Georgia, a small town in Fayette County, and laid his body to rest in the woods near a cemetery.

"You gonna say a few words, Tori?" Jamarco asked.

"Me?" I looked around at my crew. "I wouldn't know what to say."

"Say what you feel," Jamarco urged.

"Rest in peace, Morgan. You went out like a soldier."

"Rest in peace," Drac said.

"You'll always be in my heart," Dominique said as tears rolled down her cheeks once again.

"Cowards die many times before their deaths, but a real soldier tastes death only once," Jamarco said. As Dominique ran back to the car, he and Drac saluted the grave of their fallen comrade.

When we all arrived at Kendra's apartment at around midnight, I sent a text to Alvarez. It read, It's done. I thought about sending the photo Kendra had taken of Ralph body's to Bowie Calbert, DeAngelo Robinson, Cash Money Carter, and Zaquan Butler, with a message that said I controlled the supply now, but I thought better of it.

"One of them might send it to the cops," Drac warned.

"The word is out," Jamarco said and turned up the volume on the television.

"Gangland violence rocked the city this evening. APD found seven bodies at an abandoned restaurant called Journey," said a reporter at the scene. "One of the deceased was Ralph Chapman, who is believed to have been a major player in the Atlanta drug market for years. Anybody with information about the murders is encouraged to contact the Atlanta Police Department."

"We need to be ready, in case Bowie and DeAngelo come at us. They had to know that Ralph was meeting with us tonight," Dominique warned.

"We'll be ready. But I'll be honest with you, I don't think they'll do shit. Especially Bowie," I said and turned off the television.

"What makes you think that?" Dominique asked.

"I'd like to hear that answer too," Drac said.

"Simple. Bowie's doing business with us already."

"True," Jamarco said.

"His loyalty is to the money, not the man."

"That might be true, but him and Robinson go back years," Jamarco said.

I tilted my head to the side. "Then why wasn't he there for the sit-down?"

Nobody said a word.

"Some of his other people maybe, but not those two," I added.

And later that night, I was proven right when security at Club 371 called and said that Kordal Terris and Marques Sterling had driven by the club, blasting, as my men was closing the place for the night. When my security returned fire, Terris and Sterling's car crashed into a telephone pole, and they were shot while trying to escape the scene. We were able to get through that without any civilians being killed or injured in the incident.

I informed my crew about what had happened at 371. "Though there was no collateral damage, everybody needs to keep a low profile for a while," I ordered.

So Kendra and Jamarco went to visit his people in New Orleans, while Drac, Dominique, and I flew to Cali. We checked into the Torre de Cali Plaza Hotel, and I sent a text message to Alvarez.

In Cali. Let's get together.

He responded two days later.

Meet me at Beirut de la Sexta Café Restaurante in two hours.

Two hours later the three of us were at Beirut de la Sexta Café Restaurante, but Alvarez wasn't. Since we were hungry, after waiting for an hour, we ordered food. By the time we had finished eating, he was still a no-show. I sent another text message.

I'm here. Where are you?

I got no response and wondered why.

"What's up with your people?" Drac asked.

I raised an eyebrow. "No idea."

"Should we stay or get outta here?" Dominque asked.

"Let's go. He'll reach out when he's ready," I said, and we headed back to our hotel.

As we were walking through the lobby, a man approached me.

"Mr. Alvarez is waiting for you in the Maceta Café-Bar."

"Where is that?"

"In the lobby. Over there," the man said and pointed.

I turned and took a step, and when Drac and Dominique started to go with me, the man added, "Mr. Alvarez will speak with you alone."

"It's cool. Go back to your rooms and I'll get with you later," I told Drac and Dominique. Then I followed the man into the lobby bar.

Alvarez rose to his feet when he saw me coming. "Apologies are in order. I had an important matter to deal with, and it couldn't be helped."

"No worries," I said as I took a seat.

He sat back down. "So, it's done."

I discreetly passed him my phone, which display the photo Kendra had taken of Ralph.

He nodded. "With proof of your kill no less. But I'm curious to know, why you are here? Did you think I didn't believe you when you said it was done?"

"No way for me to be sure whether you did or not."

"You and I are partners now, Tori. That means we have to trust each other, or this will never work out. In fact, a lack of trust will make things go badly between us. That is what happened between my father and Ralph. After Ralph made several questionable moves, my father lost confidence in him, and the decision was made to cut ties with him. I would hate it if that were to happen between us, Tori."

"I promise you that it won't."

"Be sure that it doesn't."

"You wouldn't care to share what Ralph did that made your father lose confidence in him, would you?"

"Let's just say that he should have been more careful about who he talked to."

From that, all I could think of was the police, the DEA maybe, or even the FBI. None of the above were good.

"I understand."

But I understood clearly what that could and probably would mean for my organization going forward. If Ralph had been in bed with the Feds, or Feds had an operation up and running that involved him, they would be all over his murder and would be looking to see who had stepped in to fill his position.

Now I was especially glad that I hadn't let my ego get the better of me and done something stupid, like announce that I had killed Ralph and sent my proof of the kill to everybody. Paranoia began to creep in, and I immediately deleted the image on my phone. Suddenly I began to question whether coming here was a good idea, and I wondered if maybe the Feds were the reason why Alvarez had been slow to respond to me.

"I've taken up enough of your time," I said quickly and bounced to my feet. I turned and walked away from the table.

"No problem," he said to the back of my head.

I returned to my room and called Dominique. "Pack up and call the airport. Book us on the next flight outta here."

"What's wrong?"

"I'll explain later."

"You wanna go back to Atlanta?"

"No, book us on the next flight to Vegas."

"You got it. Is everything all right?"

"Yeah, everything is cool. We just need to get outta here, that's all."

My paranoia got worse after I hung up the phone. What if the cops or the DEA or whoever was already on me had followed us here?

How fucked up would that be?

Up to this point, I had been running a quiet program and had managed to stay off law enforcement's radar. But I had made some major moves lately, and I wondered if the law had taken notice. Did the cops know about my sit-down with Ralph?

"Stop it!" I shouted at myself. "Stop this shit right fuckin' now!"

I went to the minibar and got a bottle of rum. I opened it, drank it down, and grabbed another. I sat down on the bed. Even if all that shit was true and the DEA was now camped out in the hotel lobby, there wasn't a damn thing I could do about it. I drank the rum, got my suitcase, and packed. When Dominique called back with flight information, I calmly suggested that we head out and wait for our flight at the airport.

"It's gonna be a long wait," she said, because it was a three-hour wait.

"All good. I'm sure the airport has a bar. We'll be good and drunk by takeoff time."

"You sure everything's all right?"

"I'll explain when I see you."

Chapter 30

I was trippin'.

Trippin' hard, and I needed to get hold of myself. I told myself again that even if the DEA was now camped out in the hotel lobby, there wasn't a damn thing I could do about it. I said it again, aloud this time.

"There ain't a damn thing I can do about it."

With that renewed sense of clarity, I got up and left the room. I went to Dominique's room and knocked on the door. She opened the door, and I went in.

"You wanna tell me what's wrong?" she said.

"Yeah." I went to the minibar. "But go ahead and change our reservations for Vegas to Atlanta first, and then I'll tell you." I got a bottle and went to sit down.

"Atlanta? You're sure?"

"Yeah, I'm sure."

"Okay," she said, and then she made the call to change our reservations from Vegas to Atlanta.

"Now, tell me what's wrong," she insisted after she finished the call.

"Nothing is wrong. At least nothing that I'm sure of, anyway."

"Then what is going on? Why did you call me, frantic, and have me make reservations for Vegas and then cancel them fifteen minutes later?"

"Something Alvarez said got me spooked, and I got a little paranoid." I laughed. "Okay, I got really paranoid and started trippin'."

"I knew that it had to be something." Dominique got a bottle for herself from the minibar and sat down next to me. "What did he say to make you start trippin' like that?"

"We were talking about us being partners now and how we had to trust each other and how we mustn't lose that trust. Then he said that's what happened between Ralph and his father." I drained the bottle. "So, I asked him what Ralph did for his father to lose confidence."

"What did he say?"

"He said, 'Let's just say that he should have been more careful about who he talked to.'"

Dominique laughed. "And you started thinking about the cops."

"And the DEA and the FBI."

"I can see how that might get you feeling some kind of way." She took the empty bottle from my hand. "You want another?"

"Yeah, in a glass with some ice and Coke this time."

As she was fixing drinks for us, I saw the look on Dominique's face. What was a big smile seconds ago had turned into her contemplative look. "What are you thinking?"

"Suppose you're right. What if Ralph was talking to the cops? What then?"

I pointed at her. "Don't get me started down the rabbit hole again."

"But suppose he was. What does that mean for us?"

"Worst case?"

"Worst case."

"It means that they've seen us coming up behind him and have eyes and ears on us. They might have had eyes on the sit-down and know that we're the ones that did . . . it."

She handed me my drink and sat down. "Okay, let's just say, for argument's sake, that Big Ralph was in bed with the cops or the DEA or whoever, what do we do to protect ourselves?"

"Shit, if they're on us, they're on us, and there ain't a fuckin' thing we can do about it. If they aren't already on us, we'd definitely need to tighten up and be more careful about how we're doing business." I took a sip. "When we get back, you and I need to take a look at how we're running this business and look for ways to do it smarter and safer."

"Something else we need to think about."

"What's that?"

"Replacing Morgan."

"I was thinking that Jamarco needs to step up and fill that void."

"That's just it, Tori. I don't trust Jamarco."

"You never did."

"Nope."

"But you've never explained why. So why don't you trust him?"

"Because he's not loyal to you, Tori. It's that simple. His loyalty, if he was ever loyal to anybody, was to Freeman. If he had any loyalty to you, he would have never left."

"I hear what you're saying."

"Do you, Tori? Do you really?"

"Yes, Dominique, I hear you."

"Because I don't believe you truly do. Not only is he not loyal to you, but he also resents you, and the fact that you took from him the spot he believed in his heart should have been his. I remember the look on his face when Drac said, 'Tori is boss now.' The look went from surprise to hurt to anger. I believe that if we hadn't been there, he would have killed you. And I don't care what the lying muthafucka says. He *had* a side deal with LL."

"Okay, okay, calm down, Dominique."

"I am calm. I'm just telling you the facts."

"As you see them."

She threw up her hands. "Then tell me where I'm wrong. Name one thing that isn't true, just one."

"Okay, I admit, all you say may very well be the truth—" I began, but Dominique cut me off.

"And how do you know what happened to him while he was gone for months? We don't. He could have got locked up and made a deal to give you up."

"Okay, Dominique. I see your point, and you're right. All that you're saying is true."

She crossed her arms over her chest. "I know it is."

"So, who do you see moving into Morgan's spot?" I paused to see if I could discern whether she had somebody in mind. "Because those are big shoes to fill, and they need to be filled right away."

"I don't know."

"You mean that there is nobody. Don't you think I've been thinking about this? Well, I have. Since the second we laid him to rest, I've been thinking about how I was going to replace him, and the only one I see that knows the business and the people is Jamarco." I paused. "Tell me I'm wrong."

Dominique said nothing for a second or two. "You're not wrong, but neither am I."

"And that's why I need you to ride shotgun over him."

"What do you mean?"

"Morgan had free rein and ran his people the way he saw fit, but it's not gonna be like that with Jamarco. He works for and reports to you," I said, knowing that one of the major changes that I needed to make was to start insulating myself more than I had. I didn't need to talk to anybody but Dominique. "From now on, everything flows through you."

"Even Drac?"

"Yes, even Drac. And you don't need to talk to anybody but the two of them."

"I think that's a good idea. We all need to start limiting our exposure."

"Even if the cops or the DEA is not on us now, they soon will be, and we need to be ready for them and be running a tighter program," I said just as there was a knock at the door.

"It's probably Drac," Dominique said and went to let him in.

"All packed and ready to go to Vegas," Drac announced as he entered.

"We're not going to Vegas anymore," Dominique said and closed the door behind him.

He blinked a few times. "We're not?"

"No, we're not going to Vegas anymore. We're going home," I said and stood up. "I'm going to pack. Call me when the limo gets here, and I'll meet y'all in the lobby." I started for the door but stopped. "Go ahead and fill Drac in on what we just talked about."

"All of it?" Dominique asked.

"I'll leave it up to you on whether you want to tell him your personal opinion or not."

Dominique smiled, and then she laughed. "Oh, believe me when I say that Drac is well aware of my personal opinion about Jamarco."

"She doesn't trust him," Drac said and sat down.

I turned around and sat down next to him. "Since it's out in the open, why don't you tell me how you feel about Jamarco?"

"As long as you keep him in front of you, he's all right. But ain't no telling what he's doing behind your back. He's fine as long as Kendra stays on top of him," Drac said.

"But what about beyond that?" I asked.

He shook his head. "The man is not loyal to anything or anybody. It's all about him."

"So, you don't see him in Morgan's spot?" I asked.

"You don't have a choice. But I intend to continue to watch him like a predator watches his prey, as I know Dominique does."

"Then it's settled." I stood up. "I'm going to pack. Call me when the limo gets here, and I'll meet y'all in the lobby."

It was late when our flight landed in Atlanta, but despite that, the first place that we went was to the club. We were all surprised but not shocked that Jamarco was there when we got there. According to Kendra, they had stayed overnight in New Orleans, but in the morning, they had packed up and were back the same day.

"And he seemed nervous the entire time we were there," Kendra whispered to me when we were alone in the office.

"I see." Might be something, might be nothing, but it didn't change my decision. Not even when he dropped a bomb when he and Dominique stepped into the office.

"Good thing that I did come back when I did," Jamarco announced.

"Why is that?" Dominique asked.

"Because two of Morgan's people got popped."

"Who?" Dominique asked as I sat back quietly and watched her settle into her new role.

"Pegram and Doherty," he reported.

"Where are they now?" Dominique said.

"I arranged bail for the two of them and had them out in a couple of hours," Jamarco revealed.

I stood up. "I'm out. Make sure that we're all on the same page, Dominique," I said and left the room.

"What's she talking about?" I heard Jamarco ask as I walked down the hall.

"I need a driver," I said to Kenny and Luke. "Take me home."

They bounced up. "Happy to, boss."

Once we got outside the club, I got in Luke's car. Kenny got in another car and followed us away from the club. We had driven a few blocks when another car cut off Kenny's car and both cars crashed into the vehicles parked along the side of the street.

Luke observed the aftermath of the accident in his rearview mirror and was about to turn around to see if anybody was hurt. But then he saw two men get out of the car that had caused the accident and open fire on Kenny's car.

"Did you see that shit?" Luke yelled just as a Ford F-350 pulled up behind us. The big truck slammed into his rear end. "What the fuck!" Luke said.

"Get us outta here!" I shouted.

Luke looked back. "Here it comes again!" he yelled, and the F-350 rammed us again.

Luke stepped on the gas and tried to get away from the truck, but the truck kept coming. The F-350 slammed into the car again. The force of the impact caused Luke to hit his head on the steering wheel. Two shooters began firing at Luke's tires at the same time that the truck ran us off the road. We flipped over twice before landing upright on our wheels. The truck stayed on us and pushed us back onto the road and then into a strip mall, and we crashed into a store. Luke jerked forward and was forced back by the impact of the airbags.

"You all right?" I said when the dust had settled, so to speak.

"I'm okay. What about you?" he asked.

"I'm all right, but we gotta get outta here," I said.

I watched as two men armed with AK-47s got out of the truck and opened fire. Gun in hand, Luke got out of the car and was immediately hit in the shoulder. Luke dropped his gun. Then he caught another round in his thigh. He went down.

Still dazed from the collision, I got out of the car, got off a couple of shots, and then tried to get away from there, firing shots as I ran through the store. The men fired back and followed me into the store. I took cover and fired back at them. I saw Luke struggling to make it to his feet. He took aim and hit one of the men. The man fired his AK wildly as he went down hard. When the other man turned and fired at Luke, I fired a couple of shots and then ran out the back door. When Luke fired again, the man fired back, and Luke fell to the ground. He was dead.

Once I was outside, I took cover behind a dumpster, took aim, and waited for the door to open. When it did and I saw the man, I fired until my gun was empty, and he went down. I thought about going to see if he was dead, but then I thought better of it. I ran as fast as I could away from there. When I couldn't run anymore, I hid between some cars, got out my phone, and called Dominique.

"Somebody just tried to kill me," I sputtered when she picked up. I was breathless and was hardly able to say the words.

"Where are you?"

"Somewhere on Old National."

"Text me your location."

I sent the text.

"I got it. We're on our way to come get you."

Chapter 31

Somebody had tried to kill me.

There was a part of me that didn't want to believe it.

Even when I say aloud, "Somebody tried to kill me," it was still hard to believe.

But somebody *had* tried to kill me, and I wanted to know who. I looked out the window as we drove. Then I glanced over at Dominique, wondering how much longer it was going to take to get there. I sat up straight when we pulled into the motel parking lot. We got out and were escorted to a room on the second level. Dominique knocked once, and the door opened.

"What's up, Dominique?" Drac asked, and then he saw me. "You shouldn't be here, Tori," he said, blocking the door.

Dominique frowned. "That's what I told her."

"Well, I *am* here. Now, move out of my way."

When he stepped aside, I went into the room. I looked at the man tied to the ceiling fan, with his hands above his head and duct tape over his mouth. Drac had put a drop cloth under him.

"Drop cloth. Nice touch," I said, and I looked at the third man in the room, whom I'd never seen before. He had jumper cables in his hands, they were connected to a battery, and that was all I needed to know. "This him?" I asked, referring to the man tied to the ceiling fan.

Drac nodded. "Yup. He's one of the men in the car that had cut off Kenny. The other is in the bathroom with Jamarco."

I went into the bathroom to find that Jamarco had the other man in the shower, with his hands above the showerhead, secured with handcuffs. His shirtsleeves were ripped off, and there were two long cuts on each of his arms and a very small one on his neck. He was shaking because he was going into shock. He was starting to get cold and losing color because he was dying slowly.

"You're gonna bleed to death," Jamarco said, and I could see the fear in the man's eyes. "Or you could tell me who sent you."

I heard the man tied to the ceiling fan scream as I left the bathroom. Drac would hit him with hard lefts and rights to the face, chest, and stomach, and then his helper would shock him with the jumper cables. I sat down on the bed, crossed my legs, and made myself comfortable. I nodded at Drac, and he went back to work.

"Who sent you?" Drac shouted in the man's face, and his helper shocked him when he didn't answer. Dominique shook her head and sat down next to me.

"How much of this are you planning to watch?" she asked me.

"I'm gonna sit here until I'm tired of watching or one of them tells who sent them," I said.

But after an hour, I had lost patience. "This mutha-fucka ain't gonna tell us shit." I stood up and took out my gun. "Take the gag outta his mouth," I said as I put the silencer on my gun and walked up to him. "Who sent you?" I shouted when the gag had been removed.

"Fuck you!" he shouted back, and I put my gun in his mouth and pulled the trigger. The blast blew a hole in the back of his head. Blood splattered on the drop cloth.

"Damn," Dominique said and looked away.

I walked into the bathroom. "Take the gag outta his mouth."

Jamarco took the gag out.

"Who sent you?"

The man didn't even lift his head, much less answer. I put the gun to his head; he opened his eyes.

"Who sent you?"

When he didn't answer, I pointed the gun at his head and pulled the trigger. Once again, blood splattered everywhere; some of it got on Jamarco.

"Fuck finding out who sent them. I'm gonna kill them all," I said and walked out of the bathroom. "Let's go, Dominique."

We left the motel room and headed across the parking lot, and as we got closer to the car, Dominique spotted an Acura coming at us fast. When she saw the gun come out of the window, she pushed me to the ground and yelled, "Get down!"

Dominique and I lay motionless as bullets whizzed by over our heads. Once the car drove on, both of us got up.

"You all right?" I asked.

"Yeah. You?"

"Yeah. I'm all right, but this shit is getting ridiculous. These muthafuckas done fucked around and made me start taking this shit to them."

After that, I didn't give a fuck who was trying to kill me. I knew that I had enemies, and I knew who they were. Now I considered all the people who worked with or for Ralph or got product from him enemies that needed to be eliminated. I would see them all die.

"Shawn!"

"Who this?"

"It's Tori," I answered, trying to sound drunk and horny.

"What's up?"

"You."

"Me?"

"Yeah, muthafucka, you what's up. What you into?"

"Nothing." He sounded confused.

"You wanna get together, do some things?"

"Hell yeah. Where you at?"

"Where you at?"

"I'm at the Blue Room."

"Bet. I'ma come get you, and we can go somewhere. We'll see if you can back up all that shit you been talking for years."

"You just don't know, but you're about to find out. Bring your fine ass on."

"On my way," I said and ended the call.

Dominique laughed. "You think he's suspicious?"

"He was at first." I got up and prepared to leave. "Until I told him I was setting out this pussy. Then he was all in."

The Blue Room was a strip club on the west side. It was a big club with a couple of stages, and there was always a bunch of women doing table dances. When I got there with Dominique, the place was packed. That was perfect for what I had planned.

"You see him?" she asked.

"That's him at the bar over there." I pointed him out. "This ain't gonna take long."

As I approached Shawn at the bar, I took my gun out and put the silencer on. I kept my head down and walked right up behind him. He was tossing money at the big-booty dancer, so he never saw me coming. I put the gun to the back of his head, pulled the trigger, and kept walking. I was walking out the door with Dominique before his body hit the floor.

The following day, I followed Drac into a building, and once we reached a certain apartment, he picked the lock. There was music playing as we made our way through the apartment to the bedroom, and as we stood in the hallway, we could hear the sounds of sex. Drac opened the door, and we stepped inside and approached the bed. Cash Money Carter was so deep into it that he didn't know that we were there until we put the barrels of our guns on either side of his head.

He froze.

"Now roll off that pussy and don't try anything stupid," I growled.

Very slowly, Cash Money did as he was told. Drac looked at the woman.

"Get up and get outta here," he told her.

"What about my money?" she asked as she got out of bed and grabbed her clothes. "This pussy ain't free."

I put the barrel of my gun against her eye and cocked the hammer.

"Okay, okay, I'm going," she stammered.

Once she was dressed, Drac put his gun to her head. "Now, get outta here and forget you were ever here."

"Be easier to forget if I had some money," she muttered on her way to the door.

Drac grabbed the purse she was carrying, rummaged through it, and pulled out her license. He looked at it and handed it to me.

I glared at her. "Now I know where to find you. That make it easier?"

"I forgot already," she said and left the apartment.

Cash Money sat up in bed. "What's this shit about, Tori?" he questioned. "I didn't have anything to do with them trying to kill you."

"Doesn't matter," I said, and both Drac and I aimed our weapons at Cash Money and emptied our clips, put our guns away, and left the apartment.

Next on my list was Zaquan Butler. He always rolled with four or five guys, so it would be harder to hit him, but not impossible. The way I saw it, all I had to do was separate him from his men. I knew that they usually traveled in two cars. Butler in one car with two men, and two or three in the other car.

Once I had my people in place, we watched as the five surrounded Butler and made their way to the cars. Once he was inside the car with his two men, the other three got in the second car, and the driver of the second car pressed the button to start the engine. When he did, the car blew up and a van pulled in front of the car Butler was in to block his escape. The van doors swung open, and two men opened fire. Butler's men got out, and one returned fire and the other got Butler out of the car. Butler and his man stayed low and were able to make it back to the house. When they came through the door, Dominique shot Butler's man in the head.

"Tori," Butler said when he saw me standing there with a gun in his face. "I knew it was you behind it," he muttered before I shot him twice in the chest. His body dropped. I stood over him and put two in his head.

"Last man coming in now," Dominique informed me and raised her weapon.

"What the . . . ?" the man managed to get out before she put two in his head.

Dominique holstered her weapon. "We need to go."

"Right behind you," I said and followed her out.

As much as I wanted to, I knew that I couldn't kill each one myself. Hell, to hear Dominique and Drac tell it, I shouldn't have done any of them myself. I knew that I had said that I was going to insulate myself from the day-to-day grind of the operation. That definitely included my participation in the murder of my enemies.

Fuck that.

For some reason, I took somebody trying to kill me personally. Maybe it was my pride, or maybe it was my ego, but if there was a way for me to get close to enemies, close enough to kill, yeah, I was doing it myself.

But if I couldn't be there, I could listen as it went down. When DeAngelo Robinson came out of the building, he was too busy on his phone to notice the white panel truck that was parked across the street.

"Team one to team two," Drac said through the headset.

"Go ahead with your traffic," Jamarco responded.

"Subjects have exited the building."

"Standing by," Jamarco replied.

When DeAngelo reached his Escalade, he opened the back door and got in. As the Escalade pulled off, the panel truck fell in behind it.

"Team one to team two."

"Go ahead."

"Subject vehicle is moving to your position. You should have it in sight right about now."

"I got it."

At that moment, a late-model Impala pulled out into traffic just in front of the Escalade, and the panel truck stayed right behind it. The three vehicles drove down the street and approached an intersection. The Impala slammed on its brakes and stopped. That forced DeAngelo's driver to bring the Escalade to a screeching stop, and it barely avoided rear-ending the Impala.

Suddenly, the panel truck pulled up alongside the Escalade. A door to the truck opened, and two men dressed in black with ski masks opened fire on the Escalade with TEC-9s. The gunmen sprayed the Escalade with nine-millimeter shells. DeAngelo Robinson never had a chance.

Bowie Calbert was having dinner at a restaurant called Dynata. He had heard about the assassinations and was determined that he wasn't going to be next. When he was ready to leave the restaurant, he sent two of his men out first, and once they had given him the signal that the coast was all clear, Bowie came out. As soon as he got outside, a van pulled up in front of Dynata. The side door slid open, and two men opened fire with automatic weapons. Bowie took two in the chest before he could get his gun out. His men pulled their guns and fired back, but we had them outgunned. When the shooting started, his men hit the ground and were pinned down inside Dynata. When the shooting stopped, the truck pulled away, leaving Bowie and his men dead.

I had known for some time, because some people couldn't keep their mouths shut, that fake-ass Kishana Tirrell had sent the guys who had pulled the drive-by. The following night, she'd been at some club called Outro Lando, talking about how they had fucked up her perfect plan and how she was going to try again with better men. She found no takers. The two she had sent off to die were her cousins. She was laughed out of the club when she called herself trying to give Ralph's people orders. Since then, she'd been keeping a low profile, and when she did make a rare appearance, she was well guarded enough for me to back off and wait for a better opportunity. But her time had run out.

The hair salon was crowded and full of women trading gossip. When Kishana's hair was done and looked fabulous and she was about to get her nails and toes done, I walked in and stood over her.

"What are you doing here?" she snapped.

I put my gun to her forehead. "That should be obvious, fake bitch," I said, then pulled the trigger twice and left the salon.

Chapter 32

I had eliminated my enemies, and I hadn't lost any business. It may have been in disarray for a minute or two, but without exception, whoever stepped in the spot knew where to go for product. I had expected that there would be some repercussions for my actions, but there were none. That meant that it was back to business as usual.

Alvarez was as good as his word, and one by one, I heard from his people in Savannah, Columbus, Augusta, Macon, and Brunswick. He had handed me the state, and now that I had eliminated my enemies, I went back to insulating myself from the day-to-day and running my legit business. However, there wasn't much for me to do. I had brought Connie on to run the property management business, and let's be honest, Blaire had never really needed anything from me other than start-up money. Now that the cosmetics business was not only doing well but was also expanding into new markets, there was little for me to do other than sit back and watch.

Now that I had time on my hands and an influx of capital, I took the opportunity to look for new commercial properties to buy. As you can imagine, it didn't take me long to get bored with that, and I found myself looking for new ways to spend my time and money. I'd never been the flamboyant type; my clothes and my ride had always understated who and what I was. And as far as my business attire was concerned, I tried to keep it conservative, to the point of being prudish. I still had the white 2005 BMW X5 that I had bought when I first started out, and Tori the businesswoman still drove it. Drug queenpin Tori always had somebody to drive her where she wanted to go.

The question was, who was I now?

At that point, I was neither. I needed either to re-create myself or find a way to fit into one or the other. Dominique had her side of the house covered. My daily meetings with her generally consisted of her telling me that everything was running smoothly and assuring me that there was no need for me to involve myself any deeper than I was. It was the same when I'd meet with Connie. So, I forced my way into the marketing end of the cosmetics business. I figured that it would be harmless enough. All I did was hang out with Marcellette when she had appearances to attend and photo shoots.

Harmless, right?

Wrong.

Whether I was just there for show or not, people still saw me as an owner and kept coming to me with questions. I would answer, "What does Blaire want?" or "Well, let's call her and see what she wants to do," and that usually worked out. But on one particular day, the cameraman said that he was bringing in Sa'coya Yarrow to shoot some stills with Marcellette, and he asked me what I thought.

"Sounds great. I think they play well off each other," I said, not knowing that he and Blaire had talked about it, and she had decided that it wasn't cost-effective. I should have known something was up when Sa'coya Yarrow didn't get there for two hours after that conversation. So, there were a lot of union guys sitting around, doing nothing, until she arrived. It took a week for Blaire to see the images and get the bill.

"What the fuck! Who authorized this?" was what she wanted to know.

"Tori authorized it," the cowardly cameraman told her, without telling the whole story.

She burst into my office early that morning with the bill and the stills in hand.

"What did you think you were doing?" she shouted.

I was on the phone, bullshittin' with Marcellette. "Let me call you back." I ended the call. "Now, good morning, Blaire."

"Good morning," she spit.

"What did I do?"

"You authorized Leon to shoot Sa'coya and Marcellette."

"Wait a minute. I was there, but I didn't authorize shit. He told me what he was doing, and I told him it sounded good."

"Well, that was not what I wanted! He knew that I didn't want to shoot them together, but he tricked you to get around my wishes." She sat down. "Damn it, Tori. Do you know how much money you cost me?"

"No, but whatever it is, I'll cover it, no problem."

"You damn sure will, and in the future, unless you hear from me, you need to stay out of it," she said, then bounced up and left my office.

I started to go after her and tell her that I didn't appreciate her talking to me like that, but why bother? She was right. If I didn't know what was going on, I did need to stay out of it.

Blaire called me the next day, apologized for her tone, and explained again that Leon, knowing what Blaire wanted, had put me in that position so he could go against her wishes. But she also reiterated that she meant what she had said. If I didn't know what was going on, then I should stay out of it. Once again, she ended the call before I could suggest that she involve me. So, that was that, and I let it go.

The following day I got a call from Dominique.

"I have a problem that I need to discuss with you," she told me.

"What's up?" I asked, happy that somebody needed me.

"Could you come to the club tonight?"

"Of course I can."

"I'll explain then."

That evening I arrived at Club 371 and went to the office. The closer I got to the office, the louder the argument between Dominque and Jamarco got.

"What's all the shouting about?" I shouted over the two of them when I opened the door.

"You need to get your boy here in check!" she shouted.

"She just needs to listen to reason and recognize that it'll be good for business!" he shouted back.

"Calm down!" I shouted. "Both of you. And tell me what's up."

"Jamarco wants to do business with his old crew in New Orleans."

"It's how you expand your business, by penetrating new markets," he got in her face to say.

"You need to back up off me before I end you." Dominique put her hand on her gun in her waistband.

He put his hand on his gun in his waistband. "Bring it."

"Stop it! Both of you, stop that shit y'all talking," I ordered.

Jamarco stepped back. "I think this would be a good move for us, Tori. We push our way into New Orleans, and Shreveport will be ours. It won't take long before we control the state."

"It's a good idea in theory, and you're right . . . in theory," I said as I took a seat at my desk. "It would be good for business. But I know for a fact that Alvarez already has somebody in that market, so we'd be going against our supplier, and that makes it a bad idea."

"I tried to tell him all that, but he wouldn't listen," Dominique said, pointing in his face, before she stepped away.

Jamarco threw up a hand in protest. "Who says that we need to announce that it's us supplying them?"

"And what happens when we get pushback from Alvarez?" Dominique asked.

"We tell him that someone in the house went rogue and that you've dealt with them. In the meantime, we made a chunk of money."

I frowned. "No."

"That's it? No?" he questioned.

"That's it. No, we are not going to put the entire operation in jeopardy by acting dishonorably."

"I told you she'd agree with me," Dominique said.

"One thing that Alvarez stressed to me is that there needs to be trust between us. That's what got Ralph in trouble with them, doing shit that made them not trust him. So the last thing that we gonna do is start doing business on somebody else's turf. It ain't gonna happen."

"I think you're making a mistake," Jamarco said angrily.

"Good thing it's my mistake to make," I said and stood up. "Now, unless there's something else you need me for, I'm out."

"No, there's nothing else I need you for," Jamarco said and left the room.

"This isn't over," Dominique said. "He's gonna find a way to do it."

"It's over for now."

"Okay, but this is the shit I was talking about. The muthafucka ain't loyal to you, otherwise, he would have accepted the shit when I told him."

"Keep a tight rein on the product. If he tries to work around it, you'll know," I said and hit the door.

I made my way through the crowd to the exit and got in the old X5, thinking that maybe it was time for me to get something new. I started the engine and pulled out of the parking lot. I had just gotten off at my exit downtown and was on my way to the penthouse when I saw the blue lights coming up behind me.

"Shit," I said aloud, because I knew that I had a gun. I pulled over, got my fake driver's license and car registration out and hoped for the best, and lowered the driver's window.

"License and registration, please," the officer said when he reached my window, and I handed them to him. He looked at them. "Remain in the vehicle," he said and went back to his cruiser.

After ten minutes of waiting, I took out my phone and called Shep.

"What's up, Tori?" he said when he answered the call. "It's been a minute. How are you?"

"I think I'm about to get arrested," I sighed.

"For what?"

"Cop just pulled me over, and you know how I'm rolling."

"Not good."

"And on top of that, I got a gun."

"You alone?"

"Yes, so I can't say it ain't mine."

I looked in the rearview as another cruiser pulled up and parked behind the first one. A female officer got out.

"Now there are two of them," I said as the first officer got out of his cruiser. Once he had said a few words to the female cop who had just arrived, they approached the car. "Here they come. I'll call you back."

"Do you mind stepping out of the vehicle, please?" said the male cop.

I didn't budge. "You mind telling me why you stopped me?"

"Step out of the vehicle and keep your hands where I can see them," the male cop ordered.

I got out with my hands up. "But you still haven't told me why you stopped me."

"This will go a lot easier if you comply, ma'am," the female cop said and escorted me to the rear of my vehicle. I knew I was going to jail when he started to search the X5.

"Gun. Weed," he announced a minute later and held them up.

"You have the right to remain silent. Anything you say can and will be used against you in a court of law," the female cop stated.

"On what charge?" I asked.

"Probation violation," she said. She searched me and then cuffed me.

When I arrived at the precinct, I was booked and taken to a holding cell. It was over an hour later when I was allowed to make a phone call. While I'd waited, I'd thought that maybe I could get out of this because the cops didn't have probable cause to stop me and so that made the search illegal.

"We can argue that," Shep said after I told him my thoughts. "But do you really want to go there?" he asked.

"What do you mean?"

"Let's say we go there, and they investigate." He paused. "First off, your license is fake, and do you really want them looking at who you really are?"

I said nothing.

"The best thing would be if they simply charge you with drug possession and you do the time for the weed charge," Shep asserted. "I'll try to get them to drop the unlicensed firearm possession charge."

All I could do was agree with him. "Okay."

"See you in court."

Chapter 33

I spent the night in a holding cell and was taken to my hearing in the morning. When I arrived, Shep was there, along with my parole officer, Genesis Finley. She had been quietly pocketing five hundred dollars a month from me whether I showed up or not, so I hoped I could count on her. So, I was glad when Shep said that she had pushed for them to charge me for drug possession and had not asked for time to be added for the charge of possessing a gun without a license. When my case was called, the judge looked at my case file.

"Is there a reason for Ms. Billups to be carrying a firearm without a license?" the judge asked.

Shep stood up. "The defendant is the owner-operator of Aurora Property Management, and in that capacity, she is sometimes required to carry large sums of cash and checks, Your Honor. Unfortunately, the licensing of the firearm slipped her mind."

"I see," the judge said.

He sentenced me to eleven months imprisonment for drug possession and added a year for the unlawful possession of a firearm, and I was remanded to Pulaski County Correctional in Hawkinsville, Georgia, for twenty-three months. And just like that, it was over. I remembered the last thing I saw was Dominique come through the courthouse door just as they were taking me away. At that moment, I had the feeling that I had not only lost my freedom but control of my business as well.

I wasn't worried about the property management business; I knew that I could trust Connie to do what was right. It was my other legit business, Blaire's Cosmetics, that I had a bad feeling about. I was half right. When Blaire found out that I was in jail for a parole violation, she feared that she would get dragged into it somehow and made a lowball offer to buy me out.

Connie said Blaire's offer was laughable, and even if I hadn't given her instructions not to sell my stake in the cosmetics business, she would have turned it down. Once Blaire saw that my incarceration wasn't going to have any bearing on her and the company that we were partners in, she calmed down and retracted her offer.

Determined to make the best use of the next twenty-three months, I enrolled in the prison's GED program. Although Jenise Phillips was a high school graduate, Tori Billups wasn't. After I signed my name, I worried that they would find out that there was no such person as Tori Billups, but they didn't. When I completed the coursework, I graduated with my class. Emboldened by that success, I enrolled in an online college.

My thinking was that once I got out, I would need a fallback position, just in case what I thought would happen actually happened. With my GED in hand, I was permitted to enroll in an online college. I took a course called Marketing Strategy and Management to increase my knowledge of what we were doing with the cosmetics business. Since I was in the commercial real estate business, I thought taking a course entitled The Basics of Property Management would be a good idea. And I enrolled in a course called The Principles of Financial Management, because I needed to know how to manage money. And, yes, I did take that class with my eyes and ears open for anything that might have the slightest money-laundering implications.

Meanwhile, out in the world, what I thought would happen *was* happening. It didn't take Jamarco long after I went in to begin pushing his way into the New Orleans market in defiance of my order. He had amassed enough power and influence to do it without attracting Dominique's or Drac's attention. In my absence, one of Alvarez's people, a woman named Lucía Camila-Martina, reached out to Dominique and was now acting as a contact. It wasn't until Camila-Matina told her that Dominique found out what Jamarco had done.

"What do you want me to tell her?" Dominique asked me during visitation one afternoon.

"The way I see it, our best option is to tell her that the individuals responsible had no authorization to make that move. That the rogue elements have been dealt with, but we stand behind our people."

"That's the same shit Jamarco said we could say."

"Any other position makes us look weak," I told Dominique that day in the visitors' room.

It was the smart play, so I wasn't surprised when Camila-Martina told Dominique that no action would be taken and hinted that no resistance would be offered if we wanted to expand farther into the state.

"And why would there be? As long as the money continues to flow, why would Alvarez care?" was what Dominque told me Jamarco had said in response.

Not that I expected him to, but Jamarco never came to visit me. Connie came at least once a month, but most of the time, she was there twice a month. We'd talk about the real estate business and the classes I was taking, but she'd never say a word about my other business.

Dominique was nowhere near that consistent. She was a regular visitor for the first four months, but her visits became sporadic after she told me something I didn't want to hear.

"Drac is dead."

"How did it happen?"

"Cops caught him holding, there was a shoot-out, and he was killed."

It was the way that she said it that told me that she had more to say about the matter.

"And?"

"And I think that Jamarco set him up."

I think he set me up too.

There, I finally admitted it to myself.

I had been thinking about it for months but had never told anybody. I wanted to tell Dominique about my hunch now, but I knew her response would be to confront Jamarco with it, and knowing that it wouldn't go well for her, I kept it to myself.

"What makes you say that?" I asked instead.

"I can't say for sure . . . It's just a feeling. But Drac was smarter than that."

"Have you asked Jamarco about it?"

"No," she said, looking frustrated. "And what would he say if he did? 'Yeah, Dominique, he was getting in my way, so he had to go.'"

"*Was* Drac getting in his way?"

"They were bumping heads more than usual."

"You need to watch yourself around him, and be careful in the streets," was the best and the only advice I could give her. I knew that it wouldn't be long before Jamarco found a way to eliminate her as well.

I hadn't been at Pulaski County Correctional for a year when I got a surprise visit from Marcellette. Once she'd apologized for not visiting sooner, she told me what I'd been expecting to hear.

"Jamarco pushed Dominique out. Nobody has seen or heard from her in a month and a half," Marcellette reported.

"How do you know this?" I asked, since I knew that she had been focused on her modeling career and had been staying away from that business.

"Kendra told me."

"To your knowledge, is there still anybody that's loyal to me?"

"Honestly, Tori, I doubt it, but I can't say for sure."

"Well, do me a favor and tell Kendra to come holla at me if she can," I said, knowing that I had lost control of the business and I was powerless to do anything about it.

I still had a year left to do, and I resolved to do that time quietly and deal with Jamarco when I got out.

Chapter 34

When I got out of prison, I went to see Jamarco, and as I expected, he had taken over my house in my absence and had no intention of giving it back.

"We'll see what Alvarez has to say about that," I said, playing the only card I felt I could play with all my lieutenants dead or gone.

Jamarco laughed. "Which Alvarez would that be? If you're talking about your boy Pablo Alvarez, you'd be wasting your time."

"Why is that?"

"He's dead. His brother Jorge Alvarez is my supplier." And that was that. "But I'm a reasonable man, Tori. I know that it would be bad karma for me to let you walk away empty-handed."

"That's mighty white of you."

"Choose your next words carefully, Tori." He looked at his gun on the table where we sat facing each other.

"What did you have in mind?"

"Two million dollars." He paused. "Payable over the next eight months."

"Two mill?" I questioned. "Over the next eight months?"

"Take it or leave it."

"I'll take it." I should have shot him right then and there, but I had a plan.

"Smart play." He lifted the briefcase at his feet, set it on the table, and opened it. Then he counted out a quarter of a million dollars in big bills and pushed them across the table to me.

"But this is far from over between us," I said after counting the money.

"What's that supposed to mean?"

"Exactly what it sounds like. You still owe me money, and I plan to collect every dollar of it."

Before the night was through, I walked away with a quarter of a million dollars. But his willingness to buy me out instead of just taking my business told me that I still had some allies in the house I had built. And I would be able to build on that. And for the next seven months, I collected the rest of the money.

It was the very next day after I had collected my last installment that I went to the apartment that Jamarco shared with Kendra. There was nobody there when I arrived, so I let myself in and waited for the disloyal muthafucka to get there. Jamarco got there about thirty minutes later.

I guess he felt like celebrating, because he went straight to the bar and fixed himself a drink. He drank it down and then quickly poured himself another. This time he walked over to the window and sipped it while he looked out. I thought about walking up behind him and shooting him in the back of the head, but instead, I watched as he drained the glass and then went back to the bar. He put his gun on the bar and poured another drink. Then he walked back over to the window—without his gun. Now that he had disarmed himself and moved more than six feet away from his gun, I made my presence known.

"Hello, Jamarco."

"Tori?" My presence in the room startled him. He instinctively reached for his gun but quickly remembered that it was on the bar. "What are you doing here?"

I laughed a little. "That much should be obvious," I said, reaching in my old Issey Miyake shoulder bag. I pulled out my weapon and raised it. "I'm here to kill you."

He started backing up to where we both knew he kept another gun.

"I told you this was far from over between us," I added.

He reached for the spot where he kept a gun, and he found that there was no gun there.

"No gun?" I asked. The look on his face was priceless. "Get down on your knees and put your hands behind your head."

Jamarco did what he was told. "I was fair with you, and this is how you do me?"

"Fair." I laughed as I aimed my gun at his head. "Did you really think you were just gonna take my shit, offer me a couple of million, and I just go away?"

"We had a deal, Tori, and I kept up my end."

"Well, I'm sorry, but I'm changing the terms of the deal to something more favorable to me."

"This shit ain't right."

"Right? I'll tell you what's right." I hit him in the mouth with my gun and quickly returned it to his head before he did something stupid. "What was right would have been you staying loyal to me."

I heard the apartment door open. "Sorry, I'm late," a female voice called. And then I saw Kendra walk in.

"Kendra." Jamarco breathed a sigh of relief. "I'm so glad to see you."

"What's going on here?" she asked.

"I couldn't wait," I said, and Jamarco looked confused.

Kendra nodded. "I see this."

"Did you bring them?" I asked, and Kendra held up the nylon zip-tie handcuffs I had asked her to bring. Jamarco looked shocked when she went to put them on him.

"Fuck is you doing?" he screeched.

"What does it look like I'm doing?" she said as she got the second zip tie in place.

"Surprised?" I put the barrel of my gun to his head as she tightened the cuffs around his wrists. "*That's* what real loyalty looks like."

Kendra had sworn her loyalty to me, and it had never wavered, not once. Not when Jamarco had left me, not when I'd gone to jail, and certainly not now, when I was free and this disloyal muthafucka was trying to take my shit. Kendra was my soldier. She had told me what

Jamarco had planned when she came to see me after I'd
told Marcellette to have her come holla at me. I knew that
I'd need some money when I got out, so me and Kendra
had agreed to go along with his takeover plan until he
paid me the two million. Otherwise, I would have shot
him in the head the first night I was out.

"You fuckin' bitch," he shouted angrily at Kendra, and
she punched him in the face. He spit blood on the floor in
front of her. "How could you do this to me?"

"You did this to yourself when you betrayed Tori," she
said just as there was a knock at the door.

"Okay, okay, I'm a reasonable man. How much more
do you want?" he asked, and I got in a good laugh while
Kendra went to the door.

"I don't want shit now," I muttered.

When Kendra came back into the room with Dominique,
Dominique had a knife in her hand. She went and stood
behind him.

I gave Jamarco a hard stare. "I want you to die, muthafucka."

A split second later I shot him in the chest. At the same
time, Dominique took the knife and cut his throat. When
his body fell to the floor, Kendra put one in his head.

Okay, okay, it was overkill. I get that, but all of us
wanted to kill him, so we all did.

Now you know my story.

So, you tell me, did I do the right thing, or should I
have just gone on break? I'll tell you what I think. Naive
Jenise Phillips should have gone on break and hid until
Milton Holmes had gotten in his car and driven away.

But not Tori Billups.

Milton was right about her. She was meant for much
bigger things. She was meant to do whatever it was that
she had to do to get everything that she wanted. Tori
Billups was meant to be a queenpin.

So, if I had a chance to do it all again, I wouldn't change
a thing. I was meant to have that penthouse view, and
everybody who stood in my way was supposed to die.

That's how my story will be told.